# Contents

# Acknowledgments and Abbreviations

I would like to thank my colleagues in Durham University French Department for their support, especially Christopher Lloyd for reading the manuscript, and Barry Garnham, Jennifer Britnell, and Ann Moss for both reading and proofing. Many thanks to Irven Clark for performing miracles with software, to Enid Maxted for her patient attempts to raise my standards of computer literacy, and to Geoff Woollen for his editorial work and some suggestions on intertextuality. Finally, thanks to Chris Mouncey for his map.

Although *Vendredi ou les limbes du Pacifique* was first published in 1967, a revised edition incorporating elements from the children's version, *Vendredi ou la vie sauvage* (illustrated by Georges Lemoine), was published in 1972. All bracketed page references to *Vendredi* appearing **in bold type** are to this Gallimard 'Folio' edition (no. 959), which is now accepted as the standard text. References to the chapters of *Vendredi* follow the text's system of Roman numerals, which differentiates them clearly from references to the chapters of this study. Surnames followed by page numbers between brackets indicate works and articles by authors who feature in the 'References and Suggested Reading' section, with the year of publication specified if there is more than one entry. Frequently cited texts are abbreviated as below, with the page number of the given edition, e.g. (*VP*, 22):

*VP*    *Le Vent Paraclet.* Gallimard, 'Folio', 1979 [1977].

*VVS*   *Vendredi ou la vie sauvage.* Gallimard, 'Folio Junior', 1977 [1971].

*M*     *Les Météores.* Gallimard, 'Folio', 1977 [1975].

*RC*    *The Life and Adventures of Robinson Crusoe.* Harmondsworth, Penguin Classics, 1985 [1719].

# LES LIMBES DU PACIFIQUE

Cuba

Caribbean Sea

Barbados

Trinidad

Defoe´s
Robinson Crusoe

VENEZUELA

Pacific Ocean

BRAZIL

Atlantic Ocean

Mas a
Tierra I

CHILE

Juan Fernandez
Archipelago

ARGENTINA

Tournier´s
Vendredi ou les
Limbes du Pacifique
&

Alexander Selkirk

Falkland I.

# Introduction

*Vendredi ou les limbes du Pacifique* (henceforth *Vendredi*) is by any standards an extraordinary first novel. Awarded the Grand Prix de l'Académie française in 1967, it established Tournier's literary reputation, going on to receive widespread critical acclaim. A bestseller which has sold in excess of one million copies, *Vendredi* soon found a place in the French education system, and now features on the syllabuses of several British universities. This early success was no isolated phenomenon. Tournier's second novel, *Le Roi des Aulnes* (1970), won him the prestigious Prix Goncourt, and has itself sold more than half a million copies. Since then his literary output has steadily increased, in the form of novels, *contes* and *nouvelles,* a growing body of children's books, essays on both literature and art, prefaces, and commentaries accompagnying volumes of photographic works.

Tournier is an author who has the capacity not only to secure establishment recognition, but also to appeal to an extensive and heterogeneous readership; so what is the key to his success? The answer lies partly in his choice of subject matter, and, just as crucially, in the particular manner in which he handles his material. Tournier is not afraid to tackle big themes and ideas, from Nazism in *Le Roi des Aulnes* to Christianity in *Gaspard, Melchior & Balthazar* (1980), the legend of Joan of Arc in *Gilles & Jeanne* (1983), or immigration in *La Goutte d'or* (1985). Already, by choosing to write about those stories and myths which form an integral part of the national cultural and historical heritage, or those issues which engage directly with modern life, Tournier increases his chances of securing a large readership. More than this, he is a consummate storyteller, a *conteur* who has the skill to hold his readers, drawing them into fictional worlds portrayed with the photographer's sharp eye for detail; sensuous worlds in which acute psychological and social realism mingles with the magical — and sometimes sinister — atmosphere of the fairytale. Like the authors of the works he favoured as a child, Tournier knows the secret of injecting 'de la féerie dans le plus humble quotidien' (*VP*, 52).

With *Vendredi*, Tournier takes a familiar cultural *topos*, the desert-island castaway, as his starting-point, and weaves into his text strands of different branches of thought ranging from philosophy to ethnology, from psychosexual developmental theory to Quakerism. Add to this an element of the fantastic, a vein of humour, and Tournier's immensely rich and lyrical prose style, and the text becomes if not all, then at least many things to all readers. As Tournier himself stresses, the book is born only when the reader opens its pages:

> ... une œuvre naît quand un livre est lu, et cette œuvre est un mélange
> inextricable du livre écrit, c'est-à-dire de la volonté de l'auteur, et des
> fantasmes, des aspirations, des goûts, de toute l'infrastructure intellectuelle
> et sentimentale du lecteur. Un livre a toujours deux auteurs: celui qui l'écrit
> et celui qui le lit. (*VP*, 81)

The very fact that *Vendredi* engages with many facets of its readers'
intellectual and emotional 'infrastructure' confronts the critic with
something of a dilemma: does s/he opt for a comprehensive, but
necessarily rather superficial examination of the different strands which
run through the novel, or adopt a more specialised approach? In this
short introductory guide I have tried to avoid the sort of fragmented
commentary which results from trying to cover too much ground in too
little space, and have concentrated on six principal areas. The first
chapter examines some of *Vendredi*'s models and predecessors, and
seeks to establish a context of castaway literature. In case some readers
are unfamiliar with the text's principal predecessor, Defoe's *Robinson
Crusoe*, I have included a short exposition of the significant differences
which exist between the Defoe and Tournier texts in each of the
subsequent chapters, which deal respectively with narrative patterning
and the fantastic, the sexual and then the spiritual development of the
protagonist, the consequences of isolation, the presence of alternative
points of view, and finally structure.

# Chapter One

# The Desert Island : Myth and Model

Le cœur fou Robinsonne à travers les romans,
— Lorsque, dans la clarté d'un pâle réverbère
Passe une demoiselle aux petits airs charmants,
Sous l'ombre du faux-col effrayant de son père...

(RIMBAUD)

*Vendredi ou les limbes du Pacifique* is a revision—a new vision—of a hugely popular eighteenth-century novel. It is also an updated version of a modern myth, for that, according to its author, is what Daniel Defoe's story of Robinson Crusoe has become. In Tournier's eyes Defoe's hero is more than a fictional character: he represents 'l'un des éléments constitutifs de l'âme de l'homme occidental'. As a mythical hero, Crusoe is a vehicle for our self-examination and self-awareness: 'l'un des modèles fondamentaux grâce auxquels nous donnons un contour, une forme, une effigie repérée à nos aspirations et à nos humeurs' (*VP*, 221; 190). The concept of the island castaway continues to fascinate modern audiences; the Crusoe scenario still generates questions central to our twentieth-century existence. These questions, however, must now be framed differently. Written some two hundred and fifty years after Defoe's novel, Tournier's *Vendredi* addresses those issues raised by *Robinson Crusoe*, but does so in the light of radically altered attitudes to Western industrialised society, foreign cultures, the natural environment, religion, and sexuality.

Stepping outside the literary context, we can identify a factual historical event as a source for both Defoe's and Tournier's novels: the true story of a Scottish sailor from Fife named Alexander Selkirk (1676-1721). In 1703, two ships, the *St George* and the *Cinque Ports,* set sail for the Pacific ocean on a privateering expedition to pursue Spanish and Portuguese ships. The mission proved unsuccessful, and in October 1704 the captain of Selkirk's ship, the *Cinque Ports,* gave orders to sail from the island of Más a Tierra in the Juan Fernandez archipelago off the coast of Chile, where the ship had been refitted prior to its return journey. Selkirk claimed that the vessel was unseaworthy and refused to rejoin it, and though he changed his mind at the last moment and begged to be taken aboard, the ship left without him. Stranded alone for over four years, he was picked up in February

1709 by Captain Woodes Rogers, who gave an account of the rescue and
some details of Selkirk's stay on the island in his *A Cruising Voyage
round the World* (1712). Aware that the tale had aroused considerable
public interest, the journalist Richard Steele interviewed Selkirk and
published his story in the periodical *The Englishman* the following year.
Tournier drew directly on these accounts in the writing of *Vendredi*.
The Selkirk story is also recognised as the principal source of Defoe's
*The Life and Strange Surprising Adventures of Robinson Crusoe, of
York, Mariner,* published in 1719.

Part of the fascination of *Vendredi* lies in the three-way relationship
linking it, Defoe's novel and the Selkirk accounts. Both novelists, for
instance, extend the duration of the castaway's island stay beyond the
four years which Selkirk spent in the archipelago: to twenty-eight years
in the case of Defoe's Crusoe, indefinitely in that of Tournier's. The
Defoe protagonist is stranded on an island off the Orinoco delta, south-
east of Trinidad and at the end of the Caribbean chain (an area richer in
associations for his eighteenth-century readership); Tournier returns
Robinson to the less capricious Pacific Ocean. Incidents from the
Selkirk story which are passed over by Defoe are taken up by Tournier.
The same material may be redeployed differently by the two novelists.
Vendredi's fall from a cliff cushioned by the body of the he-goat
Andoar, for instance, stems directly from Selkirk's experience of a
similar fall as he chased goats for food:

> He told us that his Agility in pursuing a Goat had once like to have cost him
> his Life; he pursu'd it with so much Eagerness that he catch'd hold of it on
> the brink of a Precipice, of which he was not aware, the Bushes having hid
> it from him; so that he fell with the Goat down the said Precipice a great
> height, and was so stunn'd and bruised with the Fall, that he narrowly
> escap'd with his Life, and when he came to his Senses, he found the Goat
> dead under him. (*RC,* 304-305)

Defoe's Crusoe comes across an old he-goat dying in a cave, and though
there is neither pursuit nor fall (the goat subsequently dies of old age),
we can recognise some of the threatening power of Tournier's Andoar
in Crusoe's description of the beast: 'looking farther into the place, and
which was perfectly dark, I saw two broad shining eyes of some
creature, whether devil or man I knew not, which twinkled like two
stars' (*RC,* 183).

Details and incidents from *Robinson Crusoe* are reworked by
Tournier. Both novels' protagonists come across a footprint, but
whereas this horrifies Defoe's Crusoe (the print is not his), it is
perceived by Tournier's Robinson to be a sign of his dominance over
the island (the print appears to be his). Defoe's castaway discovers and
explores a cavern and hidden grotto, but the incident is recounted with

none of the initiatory or psychosexual resonances present in *Vendredi*.

Clearly, isolated examples such as these can do no more than give some idea of the nature of the links which connect the three texts. Given that this intertextual network exists, readers may wonder if a familiarity with the Selkirk accounts and *Robinson Crusoe* is essential to the comprehension of *Vendredi*. The answer is both yes and no. In a sense, Tournier's new version is fully autonomous: the nature and consequences of solitude, the confrontation of two cultures, the changes undergone by Robinson, can be grasped without knowledge of the text's predecessors. But for a richer reading of the text, and a fuller appreciation of the manner in which Tournier generates significance by remodelling material, a reading of Defoe's novel and Selkirk's story is invaluable. Only then can *Vendredi* be appreciated not just as a vision, but as a revision. Some of the broad areas of overlap and divergence will be outlined in the following section of this chapter. Further examples relating specifically to *Vendredi* and *Robinson Crusoe* will be discussed below in individual chapters.

One theme common to the three stories is that of solitude, and it seems reasonable to suggest that this aspect of island literature finds its origins in the historical Selkirk incident, fictionalised and developed by Defoe, who in turn engenders various successors. The public interest in the Selkirk accounts, and the huge popularity of Defoe's text, indicate that the climate was ripe in the early eighteenth century for an exploration of solitude as a fundamental aspect of the human condition. Already Richard Steele had added a new dimension to Woodes Rogers's factual account by pointing to the universal significance of the Selkirk story: the sailor's struggle with isolation is heroic 'when we consider how painful Absence from Company for the space of but one Evening, is to the generality of Mankind' (*RC*, 307). By the time of Defoe's *Robinson Crusoe*, the castaway has become an Everyman.

In the twentieth century, the notion of man's intrinsic isolation gains considerable importance, and is a problem of which Tournier is acutely aware. As religion, small communities, and family life play an ever decreasing role in modern society, the potentially damaging consequences of isolation make themselves felt. In Tournier's eyes, solitude is not only the lot of the castaway. We are all metaphorical castaways in an increasingly atomised society:

> Or il me semble que cette solitude grandissante est la plaie la plus pernicieuse de l'homme occidental contemporain. L'homme souffre de plus en plus de solitude, parce qu'il jouit d'une richesse et d'une liberté de plus en plus grandes. Liberté, richesse, solitude ou les trois faces de la condition moderne. (*VP*, 221-2)

Selkirk, though initially overcome by despair, 'came at last to

conquer all the Inconveniences of his Solitude, and to be very easy'
(*RC*, 305). Devoid of human company, he found his religious sense
heightened: Woodes Rogers records that 'he said he was a better
Christian while in this Solitude than ever he was before, or than he was
afraid, he should ever be again' (*ibid.*, 304). Left alone for a
considerably greater length of time, Defoe's Crusoe overcomes his
solitude by dint of hard work and a renewed faith in God. Introducing
psychological and philosophical frameworks particular to the twentieth
century into his text, Tournier explores the deleterious effects of
protracted isolation in considerably greater depth than Defoe. After
regressing to the animality of the *souille* and coming close to insanity,
the castaway in *Vendredi* is driven by affective and sexual deprivation to
a series of relationships with the island itself. His is a much more radical
spiritual metamorphosis, and one which deviates from the mainstream
Western Christian tradition.

Both Woodes Rogers's and Steele's accounts indicate that Selkirk had
with him a few possessions, including a Bible, some clothes, tobacco, a
gun and powder. His survival in the new environment remained at a
fairly rudimentary level: he built huts, ate shellfish and turtles, hunted
with his rifle until his powder ran out, then relied on his speed to chase
and capture goats. Defoe provides his castaway with a wealth of
material goods taken from the wrecked ship. The new environment is
transformed as Crusoe undertakes a comprehensive programme of
building, agriculture, domestication of animals, pottery, weaving,
baking of bread. In effect, by the end of his stay he has done his utmost
to reconstruct the mainland Western European environment. After the
arrival of Spanish and English sailors towards the end of the book, the
island is peopled and later becomes a full-scale colony. *Robinson
Crusoe* signals a victory for the mainland culture. Similarly, Defoe's
most important addition to the Selkirk story, his creation of the native
Man Friday, serves principally to reinforce Western European values:
Friday is colonised as thoroughly as the island, and his death, when it
occurs in the further adventures published in 1719, is keenly felt by
Crusoe, but not dwelt on at any length.

In *Vendredi*, things are very different. The new environment
becomes an active force which challenges and eventually undermines the
European ideology, just as Vendredi himself 'converts' the coloniser in
Robinson. The influence of the Selkirk accounts on Tournier's novel can
be detected here. Woodes Rogers notes, for example, that ' 'twas some
time before he could relish our Victuals' (*RC*, 306). The final chapter of
*Vendredi*, though, sees Robinson's both literal and metaphorical
vomiting up of Western culture. We learn that Selkirk 'had so much
forgot his Language for want of Use' that he was barely comprehensible
to his rescuers (*ibid.*); if Defoe ignores such a threat of de-civilisation,

this becomes a central concern for Tournier. Hints that the island may be considered as a potentially beneficial environment can be found in aspects of Steele's account. After conquering his depression, Selkirk enjoys a life which has become, Steele suggests, 'one continual Feast'. A description of the natural beauty of the island may well have influenced Tournier (for example, the *combe rose* incident). Steele describes:

> The most delicious Bower, fann'd with continual Breezes, and gentle aspirations of Wind, that made his Repose after the Chase equal to the most sensual Pleasures. (*RC*, 308)

This positive vision of the island environment is also revealed in Steele's suggestion that when Selkirk left the island he did so with some regrets:

> When the Ship which brought him off the island came in, he received them with the greatest Indifference, with relation to the Prospect of going off with them, but with great Satisfaction in an Opportunity to refresh and help them. The Man frequently bewailed his Return to the World, which could not, he said, with all its Enjoyments, restore him to the Tranquility of his Solitude. (*RC*, 309-310)

Both solitude and the natural environment provoke ambivalent reactions. Man as a 'social animal' regrets the loss of the company of his fellow-beings, yet discovers aspects of his identity which may be masked by his social self. 'Getting away from it all' may have a certain attraction: consider, for example, the plethora of *Bounty*-style product advertisements featuring the idyllic setting of the tropical island.

The Selkirk accounts and Defoe's *Robinson Crusoe* are *Vendredi*'s two most important models. As a modern myth, 'une histoire fondamentale' (*VP*, 188), the Crusoe story has engendered many successors besides *Vendredi:*

> On dirait que chaque génération a éprouvé le besoin de se raconter, de se reconnaître et ainsi de se mieux connaître à travers cette histoire. (*ibid.*, 219)

Although Tournier's attribution of mythical status to the desert island tale is undoubtedly valid, it requires further elaboration. The mythical status of Defoe's story is indicated not only by the vast number of versions modelled on the parent text, but also by the introduction of both the noun *robinsonnade* and the verb *robinsonner* into the French lexicon towards the end of the nineteenth century. Whilst the former word lays emphasis on the natural environment—'une robinsonnade' is defined as 'un récit d'aventures de vie sauvage, dans la nature, à la manière de Robinson Crusoé'—the latter reminds us of the castaway's solitary state: 'robinsonner: vivre comme Robinson, *dans un lieu désert*' (my emphasis). When Tournier Includes in his list of successors to *Robinson Crusoe* both Giraudoux's *Suzanne et le Pacifique* (1921), which features a single castaway, and Jules Verne's *L'Île mystérieuse* (1874), which does not, he fails to indicate that in many cases only some aspects of the central story are propagated.

In fact, many of the texts which we can recognise as successors to *Robinson Crusoe* shift the emphasis away from the survival of the solitary individual to the confrontation of Western so-called 'civilisation' and the natural environment of the island. In the case of *L'Ile mystérieuse*, we are no longer dealing with a desert(ed) island: there are five castaways, but among them, as Tournier archly notes, 'un *ingénieur*' (*VP*, 220). Verne's characters have no convenient supplies to help them with their projects, yet these are even more ambitious than Crusoe's. The natural environment itself yields up all the products necessary for its own transformation. Although Verne's work again represents the victory of man's 'civilising' powers, the potentially hostile forces of nature are revealed in the final pages of the text when an erupting volcano destroys and submerges the entire island. Interestingly, there is embedded within the principal narrative a separate incident which reveals how easily man may 'revert to nature'. A single castaway (a criminal voluntarily exiled at the end of the earlier *Les Enfants du Capitaine Grant*) is discovered by the five protagonists on an adjacent island. He has regressed to an almost bestial state, has lost his powers of speech, and is only gradually reintegrated into the human community. This is clearly a far cry from Crusoe's solitary successes.

Other texts — to select but a few familiar titles amongst many — such as Wyss's *The Swiss Family Robinson* (1812) and Ballantyne's *Coral Island* (1858), that between them spawn further Verne novels, also focus primarily on the adaptation of several castaways to the new island environment. In both cases the castaways have little trouble coping with the situation, and the struggles of the individual are replaced by the rather boy-scoutish joint enterprises of the cohesive community. Towards the end of *The Swiss Family Robinson,* as was the case with Verne's text, a single castaway is found. However, Miss Jenny Montrose's three-year isolation is rapidly summarised in the space of some two pages. She too is swept up into the community, and the text closes with the father dealing out lavish praise for 'the manner in which we supported our tribulations', overcoming challenges in a way that has illustrated 'the value of a varied education and the importance of becoming acquainted with first principles' (Wyss, 512-13).

The shift of emphasis away from the single castaway on the truly desert island threatens to reduce the psychological complexity of these novels, and to diminish also the role of the island as a place of struggle and confrontation. Another popular novel, Golding's *Lord of the Flies* (1954), a text which, like those mentioned above, has found its way on to many a school syllabus, can be seen to take a stand against the idealistic tale of community spirit and achievement. The island is re-established as a space of genuine conflict. The savagery which is set against 'civilised' values and most usually externalised in other texts in the form of native cannibals (who are always overcome) is now internalised: the only 'savages' are the schoolboys themselves, in a scenario that develops a situation already described by Ballantyne and Verne (in *Deux ans de vacances*) in more brutal directions. Although we are dealing with a group of castaways once again, solitude now dwells within the individual and the text closes with Ralph's weeping for 'the end of innocence' and 'the darkness of man's heart'. In the final pages of the text an exchange between Ralph and a British naval officer—the representative of the mainland ideology who traditionally comes to the rescue—includes a reference to Ballantyne's novel which serves to underline, and undermine, the community spirit and easy victories of earlier island tales:

> 'I should have thought that a pack of British boys—you're all British aren't you?—would have been able to put up a better show than that—I mean—'
> 'It was like that at first,' said Ralph, 'before things...'
> He stopped.
> 'We were together then...'
> The officer nodded helpfully.
> 'I know. Jolly good show. Like the Coral Island.' (Golding, 223)

Tournier's *Vendredi*, unlike many of the texts engendered by the Robinson Crusoe myth, because it is modelled much more closely upon Defoe's novel, returns to the single castaway and the desert island. Like Golding's novel, it both re-establishes (in fact, develops) the psychological dimension of the island story and turns away from the adventure story ethos and affirmations of Western superiority found in so many *robinsonnades*.

Although the texts we have been considering find their roots in Defoe's *Robinson Crusoe*, and though *Vendredi* is indeed one of many texts engendered by the Crusoe myth, it also has a place in a broader tradition. Marginal, often magical places, Utopias or harbourers of evil, islands have for centuries appealed to the imagination of authors and readers. As a circumscribed, privileged space, the fictional island is the perfect location for the creation of new worlds or the confrontation of different ideologies. In Homer's *Odyssey*, Odysseus is cast upon various islands inhabited by enchantress figures such as Circe and Calypso. Offered the gift of eternal life by Calypso, or tempted by the ideal kingdom of Phaeacia (another island), he must make a choice between the island and his homeland values.

The island as a place where 'civilisation' confronts nature is central

to another well-known text, Shakespeare's *The Tempest* (produced in
1611 and published in 1623). Like Defoe's *Robinson Crusoe,*
Shakespeare's play is thought to have been inspired by a historical
event—a wreck in the Bermudas in 1609 recounted in various
pamphlets. These accounts have certain affinities with Defoe's work.
The wreck and enforced island stay are interpreted as the workings of
Providence, and the importance of putting trust in God is stressed. Both
the historical and the fictional accounts present an unfortunate situation
in a positive light: the survivors come to lead better lives; Crusoe turns
his back on what he comes to perceive as his sinful prior existence. In
*The Tempest* too we see the island stay occasioning a beneficial change
in the protagonists: Prospero learns to overcome his passion of fury; the
usurpers repent. More important is the confrontation of the 'savage' and
the 'civilised'. Caliban is thematically opposed to both the learning of
Prospero and to the evil of the usurpers, so that we are led to ask who is
more evil, the savage or the so-called civilised men? The theme of
slavery echoes from Shakespeare to Defoe to Tournier in the image of
submission: Caliban swears allegiance to the drunken butler Stephano:
'I'll kiss thy foot; I'll swear myself thy subject' (II: ii). Man Friday
prostrates himself before Robinson:

> ... at length he came close to me, and then he kneeled down again, kissed
> the ground, and laid his head upon the ground, and taking me by the foot,
> set my foot upon his head; this it seems was in token of swearing to be my
> slave for ever. (*RC,* 207)

Before his fall from grace due to his lust for Miranda—a sexual
threat echoed in the Tournier text when Vendredi 'betrays' Robinson
with the island—Caliban teaches Prospero about the natural resources of
the island. Gonzalo, during a humorous exchange about the merits of
civilisation, extols natural values, outlining the plans he would execute
were he king of the island:

> I' th' commonwealth I would by contraries
> Execute all things; for no kind of traffic
> Would I admit; no name of magistrate;
> Letters would not be known; riches, poverty,
> And use of service, none; contract, succession,
> Bourn, bound of land, tilth, vineyard, none;
> No use of metal, corn, or wine, or oil;
> No occupation; all men idle, all;
> And women too, but innocent and pure:
> No sovereignty [...]
> [...] but Nature should bring forth,
> Of its own kind, all foison, all abundance,
> To feed my innocent people. (II: i)

Gonzalo's speech is itself modelled on John Florio's translation of

Montaigne's *Essais*. The passage in question comes from a description of the 'new world'—Brazil—in 'Des cannibales'. Montaigne's comments earlier in the same text would not be out of place in Tournier's own work: 'il n'y a rien de barbare et de sauvage en cette nation [...] sinon que chacun appelle barbarie ce qui n'est pas de son usage'.

The island is a magical realm: Prospero the magician has at his command elves and spirits which cross the sand 'with printless foot'. One cannot help but be reminded of the famous footprint in Defoe. Ariel the air-spirit heralds Vendredi and his 'âme aérienne'. The aeolian harp built by Vendredi is echoed in the music of an island 'full of noises,/ Sounds and sweet airs, that give delight, and hurt not' (III: ii).

One should not over-emphasise similarities, yet it must be said that aspects which are central to what Tournier perceives as the Robinson Crusoe myth do predate Defoe's text. Although the strictly 'desert' island and the particular idea of reconstructing aspects of the mainland civilisation on the island originate with Defoe's *Robinson Crusoe*, Tournier's *Vendredi*, as well as constituting a revision of the myth, also belongs to a more extensive tradition of island literature.

*****

A myth, says Tournier, in addition to being '*une histoire fondamentale*', is also '*une histoire que tout le monde connaît déjà*' (*VP*, 188; 189; author's emphasis). Quite how knowledge of such stories is disseminated he never explains satisfactorily. The example he gives refers to another of his novels, *Les Météores* (1975), which focuses on the lives of identical twins. In this case, the subject matter is familiar to us, says Tournier, because anecdotes of twins abound. However, though we may all have heard stories about twins, I doubt if many of us exchange tales of island castaways. As far as the *Robinson Crusoe* story is concerned, familiarity comes primarily from the many versions produced, ranging from literary successors to cartoons, comic-strips, films, and pantomimes. It certainly seems to be the case that a small number of stories capture the public imagination and trigger off a panoply of different versions in various mediums. This applies, for example, to Shelley's *Frankenstein* story, the essence of which survives (albeit in somewhat distorted form!) as popular television shows such as *The Munsters* and *The Addams Family*, joke-shop accessories (the bolt through the neck), popular music—'Monster Mash' in the '60s—and even the Electricity Board privatisation advertisements of the early '90s.

The existence of such popularisations means that the stories are accessible in their basic form even to small children, and indeed Tournier suggests that this is another quality of the myth: it is a story which operates at various levels, both as a straightforward tale which can be enjoyed by children, and at a metaphysical level. This, Tournier points out, is the case for his version of the Robinson Crusoe myth, which is both commented on by the critic and philosopher Gilles Deleuze (see the essay appended to the Folio edition of *Vendredi*), has been produced as a children's play, screened as a feature film starring Michael York in Robinson's role, and rewritten in a children's version as *Vendredi ou la vie sauvage* (1971), the most recent edition of which includes a supplement comprising quizzes ('Pourriez-vous vivre sur une île déserte?'), multiple-choice questions on the text, and games. In December 1988, Tournier agreed to appear on the *Ex Libris* book programme and judge a nationwide competition for schoolchildren to revise the ending to their satisfaction, pronouncing himself enchanted with the response. Maybe he preferred it to his own brief 'La Fin de Robinson Crusoé' (*Le Coq de bruyère*), in which the two men become drunken degenerates, and Robinson embarks after the death of his wife on a fruitless search for his now unrecognizable island. But whether all myths are accessible to children is another matter. Tournier refers to Don Juan's mythological status, yet here it would be difficult to envisage a children's version.

Of course, though the story may be one 'que tout le monde connaît déjà', the knowledge involved may be extremely limited. Most people I have asked about Robinson Crusoe 'know the story' to the extent that they recall a man cast upon an island. Some have vague recollections of Man Friday, few can suggest what becomes of him, and even fewer are aware of the text's strong colonising and moral dimensions. Knowledge of the story is thus limited to the basic situation. This is, of course, in itself indicative that to some extent Tournier is correct. There is indeed something powerful or fundamental enough about the desert island tale for the bare lines of it to be disseminated.

Perhaps we might sum up the situation by considering four factors central not only to the Crusoe story, but also to other examples of island literature, and suggest that it is these core elements which hold the key to the fascination which Defoe's text and others like it exercise:

1. **Solitude:** the castaway is separated from the company of his or her fellow beings.

2. **Conflict:** the island represents an ideological system which differs radically from that of the continent or mainland (which will usually represent the reader's own values as well as those of the castaway). At some stage during his stay the castaway may be faced with a representative of the island environment and value systems.

3. **Change:** the island stay effects some changes in the castaway.

4. **Magic:** the island harbours some form of magical or supernatural dimension.

Whilst other elements common to the corpus of island literature could doubtless be isolated, these four provide us with a useful heuristic approach to texts. More specifically, the varying treatment and emphasis of these factors allow us to compare and contrast different texts. For instance, is solitude a central concern, or is the emphasis shifted to one or more of the other factors? If we are dealing with a desert island, is isolation seen in wholly negative terms? How does the castaway overcome his or her solitude? The question of gender is itself significant: a great many island texts exclude the female sex.

Degrees of conflict vary: the new environment and the culture it represents may be viewed as wholly alien and hostile, or as potentially beneficial and acceptable. The changes undergone by the castaway(s) can be used as a means of reinforcing the mainland ideology (as is the case in *Robinson Crusoe*) or undermining it (as in *Vendredi* ). The supernatural dimension assumes many forms. In some cases it may turn out to have a rational explanation: apparently inexplicable incidents in Verne's *L'Île mystérieuse* are revealed to be the work of Captain Nemo. In other texts we may be confronted with a truly magical realm (*The Tempest, The Odyssey*). The interplay of these four factors in *Vendredi* will be explored more fully in the course of the following chapters. One of them, the magical dimension, will be seen to be closely linked to the play of narrative point of view.

# Chapter Two

## Points of View

> If ever the story of any private man's adventures in the world
> were worth making publick, and were acceptable when published,
> the editor of this account thinks this will be so.

The Preface to Defoe's *Robinson Crusoe* (the opening words of which are quoted above) reveals the author in the guise of editor urging the reader to accept the story which follows as a true (i.e. not fictional) historical incident. Narrated wholly in the first person, Crusoe's tale is presented as the retrospective account of a real castaway, set down on paper upon his return to civilisation. Crusoe is thus both teller and told. Within the text are extracts from the journal kept during his island stay, and subsequently cited by him in the course of his narration. Tournier's revision radically alters this narrative organisation. We are no longer dealing with a protagonist who supposedly returns to tell his own story in the first person; instead, the narrative is split between an anonymous third-person narrator who plays no part in the related events, and the first-person log-book which records Robinson's own thoughts and impressions. Far from introducing an editorial figure claiming that the events recounted are 'true' or 'factual', Tournier's text at times blurs the boundaries between the real and the fantastic, calling into question our very definitions of reality.

Although the two novels share the common feature of a record held by the castaway during his island stay, the nature and function of these documents differ. Robinson's 'journal' in Defoe's text becomes a 'log-book' in *Vendredi*. Ship's log-book, captain's log, the terms are associated with progress, a voyage, a spatial displacement. The renaming by Tournier foregrounds the fact that Robinson's island sojourn is indeed a journey of sorts. As keeper of the log-book, Robinson will chart the stages or ports of call not of a physical, but of a spiritual voyage. This metaphorical journey will bring him into contact with the elemental forces of nature, so it is appropriate that his writing materials should come from nature itself: red ink from the fish in the sea, blue from the leaves of the earth; vulture feathers associated with carrion and death, albatross quills procured by the aerial Vendredi. In contrast, Defoe's Crusoe, usually so adept, declares himself unable to manufacture ink, and remains reliant on civilisation's bounty. When the ink which he salvages from the wrecked ship begins to run dry (after only one year of the twenty-eight-year period spent on the island) his journal is reduced to a bare minimum of 'the most remarkable events' of his life, before petering out altogether.

The inception of the journal in *Robinson Crusoe* is as low-key as its cessation. Greater emphasis is laid on the construction of the table and chair at which Crusoe sits to write than upon the act of writing itself, indeed writing is presented as just one activity amongst others. Crusoe states: 'I could not write, or eat, or do several things with so much pleasure without a table' (*RC*, 85). In *Vendredi*, the log-book assumes an altogether more important role. Robinson regards the act of writing as proof of his humanity. It is the mastery of language which separates man from beast:

> Il pensa pleurer de joie en traçant ses premiers mots sur une feuille de papier. Il lui semblait soudain s'être à demi arraché à l'abîme de bestialité où il avait sombré et faire sa rentrée dans le monde de l'esprit en accomplissant cet acte sacrée: écrire. (**44-5**)

If the importance of writing and the role of language are reduced in *Robinson Crusoe*, it is because Defoe's hero is never truly endangered by his situation. The novel promotes the successful struggles of the individual and the civilised values he embodies. There is never any real doubt that Western European culture will prevail, nor any suggestion that Crusoe will regress to an inhuman condition. The isolated natural environment is never a genuine threat, any more than it is a possible means of liberation and salvation. In sharp contrast, Tournier's Robinson is revealed to be at risk. In spite of his talking aloud in an attempt to preserve his linguistic capacities, his repertoire and manipulation of language apparently diminish: 'je vois de jour en jour s'effondrer des pans entiers de la citadelle verbale dans laquelle notre pensée s'abrite et se meut familièrement' (**68**).

I say 'apparently', because in spite of this claim there is in fact little sign of linguistic deterioration in Robinson's log-book entries. Rather paradoxically, his expressed fears about his reduced mastery of language are couched in the most fluent and sophisticated terms. This is an aspect of the text which is potentially open to criticism. The device of the log-book is exploited by Tournier to allow for the inclusion of a variety of material and styles, ranging from philosophical speculation, through more pragmatic considerations centring on Vendredi's presence, to the imprecatory, poetic, and elegiac tone of Chapter X (which also introduces a note of synthesis and exegesis). Whilst this variety contributes to the richness of the text, it might be argued that even if the benefits of Robinson's university education are taken into account (we are reminded that 'il était étudiant à l'université

d'York'—**45**), the character on occasion sounds more like a mouthpiece
for the author's own ideas.

This is especially true of Chapter IV, where Tournier pre-empts the
reader's potentially sceptical attitude towards Robinson's flights of
philosophical discourse by having the character himself marvel at his
new-found skills: 'Ce que je viens d'écrire, n'est-ce pas cela que l'on
appelle "philosophie"?' (**89**). Given that Robinson's philosophical
speculations are couched, anachronistically, in terms of both Sartrean
and Freudian discourse—in other words are very much of the twentieth
century though the story takes place in the eighteenth—the reader may
remain unconvinced. Objections, however, can only be sustained if we
impose realism or plausibility as a desirable norm, and the anachronism,
as we shall see in Chapter Five, has an important function.

As both the journal and the account produced upon the protagonist's
return are narrated in the past tense and the first person in *Robinson
Crusoe*, the two narrative blocks threaten at times to blur together: it is
often difficult to ascertain where the journal entries begin and end.
Although the device of the journal could have been used to establish a
counterpoint between the narrator's thoughts whilst on the island and
those engaged in upon his return, this does not tend to happen. The
function of the journal is thus rather limited, and for much of the time
it does little more than record material events: 'June 23. Very bad again,
cold shivering, and then a violent head-ach' (*RC,* 102). When journal
entries are given over to a more speculative mode, there seems to be
little distinction between reflections made during the castaway period
and those made subsequent to Crusoe's return. There is scant sense of
the protagonist's self-objectification with the wisdom of hindsight, and
the fading out of the journal is thus relatively insignificant.

In *Vendredi,* a clear distinction is established between the log-book
and the main body of the narrative, marked by the shift from third to
first person, and a change in the typographical presentation. A strong
counterpoint between the third-person narrative presenting Robinson
largely 'from the outside', and the 'inside view' provided by the first-
person log-book is set in play (Robinson both narrates himself and is
narrated by a third party). Although—or indeed, because—there are no
explicit comparisons drawn between the psychic and the material worlds
of the protagonist, the reader him/herself focuses on the gap, thereby
becoming aware of a growing dissonance between Robinson's often
troubled speculations, his confessions of uncertainty and fear, and the
figure portrayed dominating and mastering his environment.

On pages 52-5, for example, the log-book records Robinson's fears
that his solitary state is precipitating the breakdown of his capacity to
differentiate subjective impression (dream, hallucination, memory)
from objective reality. The entry is marked by the character's

desperation as he feels his hold on reality weaken: 'le rempart le plus sûr, c'est notre frère, notre voisin, notre ami ou notre ennemi, mais quelqu'un, grands dieux, quelqu'un!' (**55**). This entry is succeeded by the third-person narrative describing Robinson at work: 'Parce que c'était mardi—ainsi le voulait son emploi du temps—, Robinson ce matin-là glanait'. The reader is immediately struck by the contrast. The troubled mental world of the character gives way to an image of apparently calm control of the environment. The activities of Robinson-the-coloniser are read in the light of the log-book entry. Here, for example, the reader may deduce that Robinson establishes a strict timetable in an attempt to counter his subjective uncertainties: the greater the turmoil in his psychic world, the more he will attempt to order and control his material world.

Similarly, a log-book entry noting Robinson's fears that he is losing his grip on language is followed in the third-person section by: 'Dès le lendemain Robinson jeta les bases d'un *Conservatoire des Poids et Mesures*' (**70**). Again, the act can be seen to be motivated by the fears revealed in the log-book. Robinson desperately seeks to fix and limit categories in the material world as these disintegrate in his mental world. The growing gap between Robinson the administrator, the *vieil homme*, and the *homme nouveau* who will in time cast off the attributes of the Defoe prototype, is emphasised by the juxtaposition of the third-person narration and the log-book entry. The inherently absurd nature of the *Conservatoire* enterprise, and the fact that Robinson himself fails to perceive this absurdity, are both highlighted.

Acts or events narrated neutrally in the third person assume a new value via the log-book entries. Commenting on Robinson's construction of the water-clock or *clepsydre,* the narrator states: 'il [le temps] se trouvait désormais régularisé, maîtrisé, bref domestiqué lui aussi, comme toute l'île allait le devenir, peu à peu, par la force d'âme d'un seul homme' (**67**). The log entry which follows reveals Robinson's almost frenzied desire to control ('Je veux, j'exige...') everything around him: each plant must be labelled, every bird and mammal ringed or branded. Building the *clepsydre* is not a neutral act but part of a value-laden subjective enterprise. The rather manic nature of the log-book entry is such that the narrator's description of the character's acts retrospectively takes on an ironic tone: Robinson's control and mastery are only apparent. Events which are narrated briefly and flatly (such as the reappearance of Tenn the dog, the baking of bread, Robinson's attacking the harvest with a sword) are re-evaluated by the reader in the light of the subjective responses expressed in the log-book entries.

The absence of these entries may be as significant as their presence, and the reader should be alert to the fact that in some cases Robinson does not articulate his reactions to events narrated in the third person.

Some incidents, such as the feeling of intense joy experienced as he observes the breathtaking beauty of the island (the 'moment d'innocence' of Chapter IV) remain inaccessible to the character's reflective consciousness: Robinson lives the moment intensely but does not—or cannot—step back to objectify himself or the experience. There is thus no corresponding log-book entry noting his responses.

The presence of the log-book reveals not only Robinson's capacity but also his need to articulate his psychic world. If there is no log-book in the first two chapters of *Vendredi,* it is because Robinson, wholly absorbed by the present and his attempts to escape, has neither the time nor the inclination to write. The writing of the log-book assumes a cathartic function as the castaway experiences an almost schizophrenic splitting of his identity: the *vieil homme* labours on but is beset by doubts as the *homme nouveau* struggles to emerge. As long as this 'split' in Robinson's character remains, he resorts to the written word. The log-book entries occupy the greatest proportion of the text in the early stages (taking up a third of Chapter III), reflecting Robinson's need to combat uncertainty via what is in fact another form of organisation and regulation: not of the physical island, but of his own mental world. The proportion of log-book to third-person narrative is thereafter reduced, falling away to approximately a quarter of Chapter VII and a ninth of Chapter VIII. Chapter IX marks the beginning of Robinson's new way of life. Living in and for the present, his inner turmoil is conquered and thus no longer needs to be exteriorised and exorcised. When he resumes his log-book in the following chapter the act of writing has taken on a new function: it is no longer an articulation of uncertainty and a split personality, but a reflective assessment of his progress and a celebration of his new life on Speranza.

The split narrative perspective is such that the reader is involved in a dual process of complicity (s/he has access to the character's thought-processes via the log-book) and distancing (Robinson is objectified by the narrator). Certain narrative features, such as the narrator's articulation of information to which the character has no access, emphasise the distancing effect and serve to underline the narrator's authority. Thus, for example, an exegetic remark glossing Robinson's misplaced focus on the Bible and subsequent failure to launch the *Évasion:* 'il convient d'ajouter qu'il avait été fortement obnubilé aussi par l'exemple de l'arche de Noé' (**36**). Party to the narrator's knowledge, the reader observes Robinson and his lack of insight from a critical distance. The same effect arises whenever the narrator makes gnomic pronouncements or generalisations, for example his comments after Robinson's first experience of nudity on the island: 'La nudité est un luxe que seul l'homme chaudement entouré par la multitude de ses semblables peut s'offrir sans danger' (**30**). Again, the information is offered over the character's head: Robinson still has much to learn. Two further narrative forms have a similar effect. The narrator may adopt a judgmental stance: when Vendredi prostrates himself at Robinson's feet a condemnatory attitude towards Western values is conveyed by the humorous accumulation of phrases describing Robinson's ridiculous appearance, and a single derisive adjective, 'farcie':

> Sa main cherchait pour le poser sur sa nuque le pied d'un homme blanc et barbu, hérissé d'armes, vêtu de peaux de biques, la tête couverte d'un bonnet de fourrure et farcie par trois millénaires de civilisation occidentale. (**144**)

Judgment is often filtered through irony, marked for example by the narrator's use of Robinson's grandiose title at a point when the character's uncertainties are at a peak: 'Et ce fut rempli de doutes que le Gouverneur de Speranza regagna sa résidence' (**77**).

The narrator's privileged insight into events is revealed whenever he refers forward to a future state of affairs:

> Il ne devait comprendre que plus tard la portée de cette expérience de la nudité. (**30**)

> Cette idée l'effleura, puis le quitta. Il y reviendrait. (**46**)

> Le tunnel se poursuivait par un boyau en pente raide où il ne s'était jamais engagé avant ce qu'il appellerait plus tard sa période tellurique. (**102**)

Such an emphasis on the narrator's superior knowledge once again lays stress on Robinson's ignorance. The character is objectified, presented as the neophyte with everything still to learn. This type of formulation also serves two further functions. An element of 'trust' is established between the reader and the narrator, who is viewed as a reliable figure whose statements should be accepted as fact. This complicity between the reader and the narrator becomes particularly important when elements of the fantastic are introduced into the text and the guidance of the narrator is withdrawn (see below). References to the future also function as hermeneutic lures maintaining the reader's interest and introducing a note of suspense: s/he awaits the unfolding of anticipated events and the increase in the character's comprehension of the significance of his own acts.

Readers of *Vendredi* should be aware of the fact that although the text is divided into distinct sections of first- and third-person narrative, Robinson's thoughts are not restricted to the log-book but also conveyed in various forms within the third-person narrative blocks. The character's point of view is associated with a withdrawal of the

narrator's omniscience and is typically conveyed by either the imperfect
or the conditional tense, or the suppositional use of *devoir*. Thus we can
recognise Robinson's own thoughts about the possible location of the
island in the opening pages of the text: 'le navire [...] avait dû être
chassé sur les atterrages de l'île de Mas a Tierra' (**16**). And again: 'En
outre, l'îlot devait se trouver hors de la route régulière des navires'
(**19**). Usually the reader is left to identify Robinson's point of view for
him/herself, but on occasion the matter is clarified. In the case of the
previous example, for instance, the passage cited is followed in the next
paragraph by the words 'cependant que Robinson se faisait ce triste
raisonnement' (**19**).

It is more often up to the reader to realise that certain expressed
values or beliefs are not the narrator's but those of the castaway, whose
thoughts are repeatedly communicated by *style indirect libre*. (This
involves the thoughts or words of the character being conveyed within
the third-person narrative form, with the reporting verb of thinking or
saying removed, as well as the conjunction 'que'.) For example, 'Seul le
passé avait une existence et une valeur notables. Le présent ne valait que
comme source de souvenirs' (**39**), may be taken to represent the
character's own belief at that stage ('Robinson croyait que seul le
passé...', etc.). When Robinson discovers the body of Van Deyssel on
board the wreck of the *Virginie* he initially believes him to be alive:
'Ainsi donc la catastrophe avait laissé deux survivants!'. For a brief
moment the reader shares this belief, accepting the statement as fact
rather than the character's (erroneous) impression. The illusion is
dispelled by the following sentence: 'A vrai dire la tête de Van Deyssel,
qui n'était qu'une masse sanglante et chevelue, pendait en arrière' (**24**).
Like Robinson himself, the reader has to readjust; a subjective view
must be discarded in favour of hard fact.

The co-presence of two points of view provides a rich source of
irony in *Vendredi*, and the reader should be wary of falling into the trap
of a naïve reading. Consider, for instance, the following passage
describing Robinson's attitude towards the store of gunpowder he has
secreted in the 'grotte':

> Robinson restait très attaché à cette foudre en puissance qu'il ne dépendait
> que de lui de déchaîner et où il puisait le réconfort d'un pouvoir supérieur.
> Sur ce trône détonant il asseyait sa souveraineté jupitérienne sur l'île et ses
> habitants. (**101**).

The belief that the hoarded gunpowder constitutes a comforting
potential force ('qu'il ne dépendait que de lui de déchaîner'), and the
image of power and domination conveyed in the phrase 'souveraineté
jupitérienne' are clearly expressions of Robinson's delusions. We are
aware that the island has no inhabitants: these are no more than the

wishful creations of the megalomaniac character. Only during a second reading of the text does the full irony of the passage emerge, undercutting Robinson's point of view—once, that is, the reader realises that the gunpowder will in fact be detonated not by the 'sovereign', but by his serf and one and only inhabitant of his kingdom, Vendredi.

Similar irony can be detected elsewhere in the text, for example when Robinson discovers a footprint embedded in the rock of the island shoreline. Robinson's foot fits the print exactly and we are told: 'Speranza [...] portait désormais le sceau de son Seigneur et Maître'. Once again the claim expresses the character's erroneous belief in his power over the island environment. This point of view is ironically undermined by the following words, which emphasise the fact that Robinson's mastery is far from absolute: 'Le maïs dépérit complètement, et les pièces de terre où Robinson l'avait semé reprirent leur ancien aspect de prairies incultes' (**57**).

The introduction of *style indirect libre* and conditional tenses repeatedly teases the reader. Are comments to be read as fact or hypothesis, objective statement or subjective belief? When we are told early in the text that the materials which Robinson brought off the wreck will be the means to his salvation—'sa survie dépendrait de cet héritage à lui' (**20**)—we may, remembering the Defoe story, take this as a statement of fact. Only as the story unfolds and it becomes clear that civilisation will fail can we identify this as Robinson's erroneous point of view: we are dealing not with objective fact but subjective hypothesis. Similarly, a conditional tense may be read as an expression either of fact or of resolution: 'Il reprendrait en main son destin' (**42**).

In some cases the character's point of view is more clearly signalled by deictics:

> Il négligea de dresser des signaux [...], car il ne songeait pas à s'éloigner de ce rivage où dans quelques heures peut-être, *demain ou après-demain* au plus tard, un navire jetterait l'ancre pour lui' (**22**; my emphasis).

In fact, the rescue ship will not materialise for some twenty-eight years. Once more the passage reveals Robinson's wishful thinking. It is interesting to note that in the children's version of the text Tournier removes this potential ambiguity: 'Mais il espérait toujours n'en avoir pas besoin, parce que—pensait-il—un navire ne tarderait pas à venir le chercher' (*VVS*, 17).

We have seen that Robinson's point of view is expressed within the third-person narrative blocks, but can the same be said of Vendredi's? Although he assumes the title role in Tournier's text, Vendredi remains something of an opaque character, presented almost exclusively via his actions, narrated in the third person. Living entirely in and for the present, Vendredi could never be the author of a log-book, for the

writing act presupposes the kind of reflective distance from events which is quite alien to him. Living events can never coexist with writing about them. The reader thus has no access to his mental world.

Although Vendredi's thoughts remain inaccessible, his arrival is marked by a change in the third-person narration. The prevailing past historic tense gives way on several occasions to the perfect and present tenses, both of which come closer to mirroring Vendredi's way of being in the world (i.e. in a continuous present). Direct speech is extremely scarce. Vendredi's words are recorded only a dozen times and are limited to single sentences. (His grasp of his newly-acquired language seems to vary. His speech is for the most part grammatically correct, but occasionally lapses into a more telegraphic style: 'Les vers vivants trops frais. L'oiseau malade'—**173**). On a number of occasions, however, syntactic features seem to reflect Vendredi's speech patterns. Soon after his arrival, we learn of his achievements:

> Vendredi a appris assez d'anglais pour comprendre les ordres de Robinson. Il sait défricher, labourer, semer, herser, repiquer, sarcler, faucher, moissonner, battre, moudre, bluter, pétrir et cuire. (**148**)

The exhaustive list reads rather like a careful chant of recently-acquired vocabulary: we can almost hear Vendredi rehearsing his new language. At the same time, the sheer excess—so many verbs to produce one loaf of bread—deflates Robinson's westernising and work-oriented enterprises. The sing-song repetition of the phrases 'il est bien de', 'il est mal de' on the following page again seem to echo Vendredi's own speech: we are reminded of rote-learning of the 'two times two' variety. Although there is no direct speech, the passage seems to reflect Vendredi's (uncomprehending) recitation of his lessons.

Another passage is worth considering. Vendredi has just encountered the he-goat Andoar, and talks incessantly of his adversary: 'il parlait sans cesse de retrouver cette bête'. The third-person narrative continues:

> Andoar était repérable à deux jets de flèche rien qu'à son épouvantable odeur. Andoar ne fuyait jamais quand on l'approchait. Andoar était toujours à l'écart du troupeau. Andoar ne s'était pas acharné sur lui après l'avoir à moitié assommé, comme l'aurait fait n'importe quel autre bouc... (**195**)

Once again, the repetitive, sing-song tone conveys the exuberant enthusiasm of the character's speech.

As we have seen, the reader of *Vendredi* can differentiate, within the third-person blocks, narrative forms which represent a narratorial point of view and those which represent the character's beliefs. It is this play between a subjective (character's) and an objective (narrator's) point of view which holds the key to the fantastic dimension of the text. For a text to fall into the category of the fantastic, two principal conditions must be fulfilled. First, the text should stage events which seem to break the rules of everyday reality. The fantastic involves a transgression of boundaries: between life and death, the animate and the inanimate, the organic and the inorganic. In some texts, these events will, as the text unfolds, acquire a natural explanation or will conversely be accepted by the reader as supernatural. The truly fantastic text eschews such solutions, causing the reader to 'hesitate between a natural and a supernatural explanation of the events described' (Todorov, 33). Bearing in mind these two basic elements, we can consider two groups of examples, the first of which may be termed *flirting with the fantastic*.

Early in the text, Robinson comes across a tree stump. As he looks at it 'peu à peu l'objet se transforma dans la pénombre verte en une sorte de bouc sauvage' (**17**). But as he rationally notes in a log-book entry in Chapter IV, 'c'était absurde, une souche ne remue pas' (**99**). And indeed we are not dealing here with anything supernatural. The stump does not literally metamorphose into a goat; Robinson simply misinterprets, then reassesses his visual data. What he took to be a stump turns out to be a wild animal. There is no genuine crossing of boundaries between the animate and inanimate.

When, in Chapter II, Robinson's troubled mind conjures up the hallucinatory image of a galleon, the reader is initially lured into sharing (i.e. accepting as 'real' within the parameters of the story) the objects of this subjective point of view. The vision begins when Robinson, immersed in the *souille*, hears music, and believes it to be 'de la musique du ciel' (**40**). This supernatural reading, however, is dispelled by the offer of an alternative: 'Mais, en levant la tête, il vit pointer une voile blanche à l'est de l'horizon'. The reader is lured by the author's sleight of hand into accepting that a ship is indeed offshore. The narrator says nothing to suggest that this is no more than an hallucination, indeed, the objective description of Robinson leaping about the shore serves only to reinforce the reader's acceptance of the presence of the galleon: 'personne ne paraissait voir le naufragé'. (Only subsequently does the irony of this statement emerge—there is, of course, no-one there to see Robinson.) Again, we are only skirting around the fantastic: the scene is revealed to be an hallucination before we learn that the girl on board is Robinson's dead sister, Lucy. The transgression of the boundary between life and death is thus only a mirage, reinterpreted by the reader (and the character) as a symptom of stress, and thereby explained away.

A final example from this group comes closer to the fantastic, though in this case too an apparent crossing of boundaries has a rational explanation. Lying beneath the cedar tree, Robinson feels something move beneath his fingers, initially assumes that it is a mole, then believes that the roots themselves are clawing upwards out of the earth:

> La terre remua derechef et quelque chose en sortit. Quelque chose de dur et froid qui demeurait fortement ancré dans le sol. Une racine. Ainsi donc pour couronner cette journée effrayante, les racines prenaient vie et saillaient d'elles-mêmes hors de terre! Robinson, résigné à toutes les merveilles, fixait toujours les étoiles à travers les branches de l'arbre. C'est alors qu'il vit sans erreur possible toute une constellation glisser d'un coup vers la droite. **(189)**

This time the reader is more hesitant. S/he may identify the *style indirect libre* which conveys Robinson's own interpretation of events (the animation of the tree root), but is lured into an acceptance of a supernatural phenomenon by the narrator's unequivocal statement 'il vit sans erreur' ('il crut voir' would have cast doubt on Robinson's judgment). Until the rational explanation is provided—the tree is falling down; it, not the stars are moving—s/he may, like Robinson, accept that s/he is reading of a world of 'merveilles' where trees can come to life. The ambiguity, however, is dispelled as the reading proceeds.

In contrast to these flirtings and skirtings, we can consider three aspects of Robinson's experiences and suggest that these fall more squarely into the true realm of the fantastic: the discovery of a footprint on the rocky shoreline; the apparent 'birth' of mandrakes subsequent to Robinson's sexual activities in the *combe rose*, and the claims made in the penultimate chapter that he has not aged whilst on Speranza.

When Defoe's Crusoe discovers a footprint in the sand, his immediate response is one of almost paralysing fear:

> How it came hither I knew not, nor could in the least imagine. But after innumerable fluttering thoughts, like a man perfectly confused and out of my self, I came home to my fortification, not feeling, as we say, the ground I went on, but terrify'd to the last degree, looking behind me at every two or three steps, mistaking every bush and tree, and fancying every stump at a distance to be a man. (*RC*, 162)

Believing at first that the print might be the Devil's work, he dismisses this hypothesis in favour of a no less alarming alternative: 'that it must be some more dangerous creature, viz. that it must be some of the savages of the main land over-against me' (*ibid.*, 163). After remaining hidden in his fortified home for several days, he ventures abroad again to check if the print might be his own, only to ascertain, to his further alarm, that it is not.

In *Vendredi*, the footprint is Robinson's, embedded not in the soft sand but 'enfonceé dans la roche même' (**57**). The reader is offered no explanation for this apparently extraordinary phenomenon. Is Robinson simply mistaken; is the print sunk into clay rather than rock? Or has

Robinson indeed been on the island for such an extensive period of time that the soft deposits of the shoreline have fossilised into solid rock?

In the case of the sprouting mandrakes, the reader again hesitates between a supernatural and a natural explanation of events. If s/he accepts that Robinson's sperm has fertilised the island, which subsequently—or more properly, consequently—gives birth to the mandrakes, then s/he must also accept that boundaries between the animal (human) and vegetal realms have been crossed. The mandrake plant, whose roots take the form of a human trunk and legs, has strong cultural associations. Throughout history it has been attributed with magical properties, regarded as a healing plant and an aphrodisiac. It is said that mandrakes grow at the foot of gibbets where the sperm of hanged men falls; that they cry out like a human being when torn from the ground. The plant has strong mythical associations: mandrakes spring up where the blood or sperm of ancestral gods or giants seep into the earth. The plant harks back to a mythical age when the earth itself had the power to engender human beings; when there were no barriers between the realms of man, animal and plant (see Bouloumié, 1987).

The appearance of the mandrakes in *Vendredi* can be read as a magical, mythical event, marking another stage in Robinson's ever closer relations with the island. And yet a natural explanation cannot be ruled out. Could it not be mere coincidence that the plants grow where Robinson has lain with Speranza? There is no reason why the mandrake plant should not grow on the island, in fact Tournier researched the flora of the archipelago in order to ascertain that it did (*VP*, 116-17).

The tension between these two readings is maintained by the play of narrative point of view. The narrator, who as we saw above elsewhere flaunts his insight and knowledge, on this occasion remains non-committal, neither corroborating nor undermining the suggestion that the mandrakes are the direct result of Robinson's act. He simply states:

> Il fallut près d'une année à Robinson pour s'apercevoir que ses amours provoquaient un changement de végétation dans la combe rose. (**136**)

The following interpretation of the incident is presented in the imperfect tense of *style indirect libre,* leaving the reader to decide whether these are the ravings of a madman, or whether Robinson's beliefs should be taken as fact:

> C'était bien cela, ses amours avec Speranza n'étaient pas demeurées stériles: la racine charnue et blanche, curieusement bifurquée, figurait indiscutable-ment le corps d'une petite fille. (**137**)

Are we dealing with a supernatural co-operation between man and earth or not? Although the humorous picture of Robinson replanting the

mandrake he has examined 'comme on borde un enfant dans son lit' -
(**138**) may tilt the balance in favour of interpreting the whole incident
as mere coincidence (and a sign of the character's delusions), the
ambiguity remains. Is the union of man and island not also revealed on
the same page, when Robinson 'constata que sa barbe en poussant au
cours de la nuit avait commencé à prendre racine dans la terre'? And
what are we to make of the hybrid striped mandrakes which apparently
grow where Vendredi has imitated Robinson's sexual act?

The silence of the narrator is also the key to the uncertainty
surrounding Robinson's claims that, contrary to the laws of nature, he
has not aged in the course of the twenty-eight years spent on the island:

> Ainsi s'il n'avait pas fait naufrage sur les récifs de Speranza, il serait
> presque quinquagénaire. Ses cheveux seraient gris, et ses articulations
> craqueraient. Ses enfants seraient plus vieux qu'il n'était lui-même quand il
> les avait quittés, et il serait peut-être même grand-père. Car rien de tout cela
> ne s'était produit. (**246**)

Once again we seem to enter the realm of the supernatural. The island,
like that of Calypso in the *Odyssey*, offers up eternal life. Or does it?
The claims that Robinson has not aged are not corroborated by the
narrator; it is once again the character who interprets events. Perhaps
this is just a case of 'you're only as old as you feel'...

In the realm of the literary fantastic there are no simple answers. A
naturalistic reading which dismisses the mandrakes and Robinson's
claims of eternal youth as the delusions of a lunatic is as reductive as a
supernatural interpretation of these events. In a sense, it is not the
answers to such questions which matter but the very fact that we are
encouraged to ask them. The inherent ambiguities of the text prompt us
to reflect upon our own conception of reality, to look more carefully at
our desire to establish fixed parameters of 'normality'. Our reluctance
to embrace the fantastic is perhaps symptomatic of our rationalist,
technological age. *Vendredi* represents a challenge to such views,
seeking, amongst other things, to open our eyes to the possibility of
breaking down fixed categories and parameters. Chapters Four and Five
of this study will examine the ways in which sexual and cultural norms
are called into question; the next chapter focuses on the means by which
the text invites us to adopt a more flexible stance towards spiritual
matters.

# Chapter Three

# Spiritual Worlds

And that simplest Lute,
Plac'd length-ways in the clasping casement, hark
How by the desultory breeze caress'd,
Like some coy Maid half-yielding to her Lover,
It pours such sweet upbraidings, as must need
Tempt to  repeat the wrong.

(COLERIDGE)

In the italicised prologue to *Vendredi*, we learn from one of Captain Van Deyssel's trenchant and rather pointed remarks that, like so many of his contemporaries, Robinson set out on his seafaring 'pour tenter fortune dans le nouveau monde' (**8**). By the closing stages of the text, however, Robinson observes his fellow-sailors with the detached interest of an entomologist studying the curious habits of so many scurrying insects. The final page of the text finds him exulting in the rejuvenating powers of the *extase solaire,* Captain Hunter's worldly tales of war and conquest already a fading memory. Clearly Robinson has come a long way, though in literal terms he has, of course, gone precisely nowhere. In both Defoe's *Robinson Crusoe* and Tournier's revision, the *physical* voyaging of the central character may be cut short, but his translocation to a geographical New World marks the beginning of a journey to a new *spiritual* realm. The island becomes a space of transformation, but the nature of the changes undergone by the protagonist, and the part played by the physical location in each text, are markedly different.

Some ten months after he is shipwrecked on the island, Defoe's Crusoe is awakened by a feverish dream in which a man, 'all over bright as a flame', with a 'countenance [...] most inexpressibly dreadful, impossible for words to describe' (*RC,* 102), berates him for the sinful life he has led and threatens him with death:

> I heard a voice so terrible, that it is impossible to express the terror of it; all that I can say I understood, was this: 'Seeing all these things have not brought thee to repentance, now thou shalt die...' (*ibid.,* 103)

As Crusoe readily acknowledges, he had had no religious inclinations before this incident occurred:

> I do not remember that I had in all that time one thought that so much as
> tended either to looking upwards towards God, or inwards towards a
> reflection upon my own ways... (*ibid.*)

The wrathful figure in the dream vision proves to be a catalyst for
change. Shaken by the experience, the repentant castaway modifies his
ways, praying and reading the Bible daily. From this point on the text is
punctuated by lengthy introspective passages charting Crusoe's scrutiny
of his moral and religious development. The spiritual world which he
discovers is a Christian, more specifically a Puritan world, in which the
Scriptures play a crucial part and man, tainted by original sin
(symbolised in Crusoe's case by the 'sin' of disregarding his father's
wishes when he first set sail from England), may be saved only through
repentance, and faith in Christ as Mediator and Redeemer.

*Robinson Crusoe* presents, and promotes, an extremely limited vision
of religion. Although Crusoe himself, as a Puritan, opposes one branch
of the mainland religion—the orthodox Church of England—it is still a
single faith, Christianity, which is reinforced throughout the text,
established as the norm to which a number of the characters submit.
When Crusoe is joined by Man Friday, he converts him to Christianity
with true missionary zeal, the conversion serving to deepen his own
growing beliefs. Renouncing his tribal god Benamuckee, Friday
embraces his new religion with great enthusiasm, going so far as to
reassure his Master that if they were to make contact with Friday's
tribe, it too would doubtless be converted:

> 'You do great deal much good', says he, 'you teach wild mans be good
> sober tame mans;  you tell them know God, pray God, and live new life.'
> (*RC*, 227)

Earlier in the novel, prior to the shipwreck, another incident is used to
the same end. After he has escaped from slavery at the hands of the
Moors, Crusoe sells a young Muslim boy, Xury, to the captain of a
Portuguese ship on the understanding that the boy will be released from
slavery in ten years' time—if he converts to Christianity. Xury,
unsurprisingly, is quick to agree to his part of the bargain. Towards the
end of the text, the emphasis on religious matters becomes less marked
as the focus shifts away from the new spiritual world to the
geographical New World. When Crusoe is joined by the English sailors
and the Spaniards who are to populate the nascent island colony, the
spiritual dimension is to some extent superseded by the mainland-
oriented adventure-story ethos. Crusoe has carefully set aside gold and
silver pieces from the wreck. His plantation has prospered in his
absence. He sets out on further adventures a wealthy man.

Unlike his predecessor, Tournier's Robinson is already a religious man when he puts to sea, though, as we learn early in the text, he has been brought up not as a Puritan but in the Quaker tradition, a nonconformist—some would say heretical—sect founded in the mid-seventeenth century by George Fox. Tournier's decision to depart from the model of *Robinson Crusoe* and make a Quaker of his castaway may be partly explained by the fact that the events in *Vendredi* take place in the mid-eighteenth century, one hundred years after Defoe's tale, at a time when Puritanism was no longer the powerful force it had been in the previous century. But there is more to it than this. If we consider what we learn of Robinson's religious stance, we realise that before any mention is made of his Quakerism, one particular factor is stressed: his purity. Tournier, we know, takes a dim view of that side of religion—any religion—which seeks to suppress the physical or sexual nature of man. Condemning what he refers to as the 'phobie antiérotique' of Western religion, he dreams of an ideal Church which would be 'fastueuse, subtile, érotique...' (*VP*, 65). It therefore comes as no surprise that in *Vendredi*, purity—if we take this term to suggest a renunciation of the body, or indeed a duality of thought which places the physical in a dichotomous or subservient relationship to the spiritual—is seen as a failing and not as a positive attribute. When Van Deyssel refers to Robinson as 'pieux, avare et pur', all three terms of the description are intended as criticism rather than praise, and the captain's last words, intoned as the *Virginie* (the name, with its connotations of purity, is itself significant) founders, serve as a grave warning: ' "Gardez-vous de la pureté. C'est le vitriol de l'âme" ' (14).

If Tournier emphasises Robinson's purity at the start of the text he does so in order to stage a transformation. Repeatedly in *Vendredi*, situations are set up only to be reversed, positive values often emerging from the subversion of, or deviation from, initial positions. The Quakers, who were strongly influenced by the Puritans, were thought of as an ascetic, austere sect, speaking plain words, wearing plain clothes, shunning frivolities of any kind. In the course of *Vendredi* we see Robinson deviate from his initially puritanical attitudes until the realms of the spiritual and the physical are reconciled. But the author's desire to point to, and then subvert, what he perceives as the iniquity of a dichotomous relationship between body and spirit only goes some way towards explaining his decision to make Robinson a Quaker. The more powerful motive behind Tournier's choice of Quakerism lies in the sect's belief in the all-important part played by the Holy Ghost in the relationship between man and God. Rejecting all church hierarchy, the Quakers maintained (and still maintain) that the presence of God dwells within each and every individual: God can be known, in Fox's own words, 'without the help of any man, book or writing', His presence revealed by the 'inner light' or 'word' of the Holy Ghost. By the late seventeenth century the sect had expanded overseas, and although it became increasingly formalised, the belief in the 'indwelling God', 'the linking of man with God through the presence in every man of the Holy Spirit' remained fundamental to the faith (Hubbard, 21; 69). Significantly, this is one aspect of Robinson's spiritual position which, though tested, is not subverted in *Vendredi.*

Although, as we shall see, the Holy Ghost is to maintain a significant presence throughout the text, one of the first changes which Robinson undergoes on the island in fact aligns him more closely with Defoe's hero. Unlike the Puritans, who came to be known as 'the people of the Book', the Quakers lent considerably less weight to the Scriptures: Robinson's mother is typical in her rejection of the Bible as a text 'dicté par Dieu certes', but written by men and thus subject to 'les vicissitudes de l'histoire et les injures du temps' (**107**). We learn early on that Robinson himself 'n'avait jamais été un grand lecteur des textes sacrés', preferring to listen to the 'parole intérieure', the voice of 'l'Esprit Saint'. And yet in spite of this, he finds himself turning to the Bible which he has rescued from the ship as 'le seul viatique spirituel' to hand (**26**). This action, which represents a temporary shift away from his Quaker roots, proves to be something of a mixed blessing.

In *Robinson Crusoe,* the Scriptures provide a constant source of authority and comfort; in *Vendredi,* their role is less straightforward. It is Robinson's focus on the biblical story of Noah's Ark ('qui était devenue pour lui comme l'archétype de l'*Évasion*' — **36**), which is at least partly responsible for his failure to launch his escape vessel. The floating of the Ark was facilitated by a flood; Robinson's ship, in the absence of such a deluge, remains high and dry. If on this occasion Robinson's turning to the Bible proves disastrous (in his eyes), it is his failure to perceive a biblical parallel which later prevents him from realising that his best course of action is to remain exactly where he is. Believing that he sees a ship offshore, Robinson hurries to light the rescue beacon he has devised by piling dead wood into the hollow trunk of a eucalyptus tree. The ship proves to be a product of his imagination, and, swimming out to sea, he nearly drowns before he is washed ashore a second time, drawn by the flames of his own beacon. The biblical echo this time may be detected by the reader, if not by Robinson: just as a moving column of fire and smoke led the Hebrews to the Promised Land, so the stationary column of flame from the eucalyptus indicates that Robinson has already reached his Promised Land (see Petit, 1984).

One of the lessons to be drawn from Robinson's attention to the Scriptures is that the act of exegesis may be a hazardous one: individual interpretation may be misguided, whether wilfully or unintentionally; the written word—especially when taken out of context—is susceptible to the manipulation of the interpreter. On a number of occasions

Robinson uses the Bible to serve his own ends, as he seeks to condone actions which are overtly indefensible. When his anger with Vendredi reaches a peak, a text from Isaiah seems to suggest—to him—that his fury is justified: 'D'ailleurs, depuis quelque temps, chaque fois qu'il ouvrait la Bible, il entendait gronder le tonnerre de Yahweh'(174). By indirectly comparing himself to God, Robinson displays both his megalomaniac tendencies and his continued self-deception. He attempts to rationalise his behaviour, and stubbornly resists the evidence before him: that he should accept Vendredi and the way of life he can offer. On other occasions the biblical message is so unambiguous that Robinson is forced to question his own attitudes. When he seeks approval for his misanthropic reactions to Vendredi, a text from *Ecclesiastes* ('*Mieux vaut vivre à deux que solitaire*'—168) points him in the right direction: the need for companionship, the joys of friendship, are values which are reinforced at the close of the text by the arrival of Jaan. Similarly, it is Robinson's memory of the story of Cain and Abel which prevents him from beating Vendredi to death (177).

If Robinson frequently goes wrong when he turns to the Bible, it is because he is motivated in his interpretations by the dictates of the *vieil homme:* he sees only what the Western coloniser wishes to see, developing selective myopia whenever what he finds displeases him. The Bible thus offers him only limited consolation. Spiritual guidance, however, is available in a different form; not from the written word, but from the island and Robinson himself, or more specifically, from the *homme nouveau* who strives to break out of the chrysalis of the Western-oriented *vieil homme*. As he builds the *Évasion*—significantly, before his thoughts turn to Noah's Ark—Robinson is interrupted in his labours by a sudden downpour. Stripping off his clothes, he experiences a rush of elation: 'Il se sentait soudain en vacances, et un accès de gaieté lui fit esquisser un pas de danse' (29). As he urinates in the rain, he feels that he is participating in the elemental forces of nature, and his escape projects are momentarily forgotten. At this stage, however, Robinson fails to see the significance of his own feelings. The colonising mentality of the *vieil homme* prevails, and his brief moment of happiness is soon forgotten. It is only the reader who interprets the signs correctly. Though Robinson experiences moments of spiritual communion with the island, he cannot as yet comprehend the significance of such moments.

On a number of occasions in the course of the first half of *Vendredi,* such moments of communion with the natural world pierce through the daily grind of routine established by Robinson-the-administrator. Whilst he redoubles his efforts to dominate and regulate his environment, drawing up a penal code and legislative charter, signs that the island may offer up an alternative spirituality and salvation are there to be read. On the point of pursuing yet another absurd project—'déterminer les peines frappant l'outrage public à la pudeur sur le territoire insulaire et les eaux territoriales'—Robinson is suddenly struck by the awe-inspiring beauty of his surroundings. Once again the emphasis is on harmony:

> Or rien ne chantait pour l'heure plus harmonieusement que cette mer de feuillages contre la toile océane tendue jusqu'au ciel. Le soleil, la mer, la forêt, l'azur, le monde entier étaient frappés d'une telle immobilité que le cours du temps aurait paru suspendu sans le tic-tac mouillé de la clepsydre. (**74**)

Significantly, this privileged moment is associated with timelessness, heralding the sense Robinson will have in the closing stages of the text of living in an eternal, ever-renewed, present. Passages such as these, describing moments when Robinson seems to participate in the natural world and be in perfect harmony with it, represent steps along a spiritual path. For a short space of time the westernised and westernising *gouverneur* cedes his place to the *homme nouveau*. On this occasion, Robinson himself appears to be at least partly aware of the spiritual nature of his experience as, moved by the spectacle, he appeals for a manifestation of the Holy Ghost:

> 'S'il est une circonstance privilégiée, pensa Robinson, où l'Esprit Saint doit manifester sa descente en moi, législateur de Speranza, ce doit être un jour comme celui-ci, une minute comme celle-ci.' (**74**)

His words, however, reveal that the *vieil homme* is still very much to the fore—Robinson casts himself in the role of *législateur*—and his pride is punished when his wish is ironically granted by the appearance of a column of smoke: a sign not of the Holy Ghost, but of the presence of cannibals burning human flesh. Robinson still has a long way to go: the Holy Ghost will manifest itself only in the closing pages of the text.

So far, we have seen that Robinson's spiritual life is split between his Bible readings and fleeting, but increasingly acute feelings of participation in the harmony of the natural environment. Though these are moments when the whole of creation seems to be revealed with all the force of an epiphany, Robinson's spiritual development can be linked more particularly to the four elements: water, earth, air, and fire. In the opening two chapters it is the *vieil homme* who directs his attention to the sea (water) and escape from the island: 'Tournant le dos obstinément à la terre, il n'avait d'yeux que pour la surface bombée et métallique de la mer' (**21**). When his projects fail, he turns to the land or earth ('tournant le dos au grand large, il s'enfonça dans les éboulis semés de chardons d'argent qui menaient vers le centre de l'île'—**42**), both in the guise of *vieil homme* or farmer and administrator, and as the *homme nouveau* who penetrates the island in the *grotte* and the *combe rose*. As we shall see in the following chapter, Robinson's 'relationship' with the earth, or body of Speranza, whilst representing a certain progress along a path of communion with the natural elements, is still marked by a pattern of dominance and submission which precludes a truly spiritual union. To progress to the final element—fire—Robinson requires the presence of Vendredi, but before such a development takes place he experiences something of a relapse.

When Vendredi first arrives, the Robinson of old re-emerges with a vengeance, far outdoing his predecessor in his intolerance and bigotry. In a typical display of ethnocentric narrow-mindedness, Robinson states in his log-book that if he has elected to name Vendredi after a day of the week it is because the Indian is not worthy of the honour and dignity of a Christian name. In fact, he comments, he is hardly a human being at all: the name of an inanimate object might have been more appropriate (147).The reasons given by Defoe's Robinson are less patronising: 'I made him know his name should be Friday, which was the day I saved his life; I called him so for the memory of the time' (RC, 209).

In a marked detour away from the spiritual path which was leading him to a communion with the elements, and away too from the roots of a Quaker faith which dispensed with all church hierarchy, Robinson assumes the role of *pasteur* and delivers solemn sermons to Vendredi, the one and only member of his congregation. The absurdity of his actions is emphasised when we learn that Vendredi is obliged to kneel in the left-hand aisle of the church, the right aisle being reserved for the (non-existent) women! (150). In *Robinson Crusoe,* Robinson marvels at the power of the Scriptures: 'how infinite and inexpressible a blessing it is, that the knowledge of God, and of the doctrine of salvation by Jesus Christ, is so plainly laid down in the word of God'. The power of the Bible is such that 'the same plain instruction sufficiently served to the enlightening this savage creature, and bringing him to be such a Christian, as I have known few equal to him in my life' (RC, 222; 223). The situation in *Vendredi* could not be further removed from this. Faced by Robinson's pedagogic bombardment, Vendredi is far from compliant, responding to his master's religious instruction with barely concealed shrieks of laughter, the ultimate goad to one who is already doubting. Laughter, as Tournier points out (paraphrasing Bergson), comes as a response to a display of inappropriately fixed and rigid behaviour:

> Le rire est le remède à cette sclérose. Le rire fait mal. C'est le châtiment que tout témoin est invité à infliger à son semblable lorsqu'il le prend en flagrant délit d'automatisme inadapté. C'est un rappel à l'ordre, ou plutôt c'est l'inverse, c'est un rappel au désordre qui est vie, remise en question permanente de l'ordre d'hier. (VP, 196)

Throughout Chapters VII and VIII, we see the letter of the law prevail over the spirit, and Robinson's stubborn ethnocentrism mocked. Although, in a moment of supreme irony, he beats Vendredi into a simulated acceptance of the existence of a benevolent God, the Christian missionary ethos which prevails in *Robinson Crusoe* is powerfully undermined: there is to be no willing convert here (**149**). In fact, when the exploding gunpowder destroys Robinson's westernised system in its entirety, the pupil / teacher roles are reversed as Robinson continues his spiritual journey under the tutelage of Vendredi.

Significantly, even before the Bible is physically removed by the blast, Robinson has decided to reject it as part of the irrelevant 'messages bavards' of human society, resolving to turn instead to 'l'univers inhumain, élémentaire, absolu' to which he believes Vendredi holds the key (**179**). Whilst this decision might seem to represent a rejection of Christianity in favour of the as yet unspecified 'règne solaire', it is important that we note what it is that prompts Robinson's move: 'La parole qui est en lui et qui ne l'a jamais trompé lui balbutie à demi-mot qu'il est à un tournant de son histoire' (*ibid.*). As previous references to *la parole* have all indicated the presence of the Holy Ghost, we must conclude that it is this third person of the Trinity, so crucial to the Quaker faith, which steers Robinson towards the elemental spirituality which stems from the island itself.

Only now is Robinson able to progress further as Vendredi, shooting arrows into the sky in the hope that they will fly forever, transforming the body of the goat Andoar (later identified by Robinson as a symbol of his own telluric self) into a kite and an aeolian harp whose only instrumentalist is the wind, turns him away from earth to air. After the explosion, symbols of ascension signal Robinson's spiritual progress: the *grotte* becomes the vertical, rocky *chaos;* he climbs trees and conquers his fear of heights, scaling a cliff to rescue Vendredi. Prior to the explosion he had compared reading the Bible to a physical experience:

> Ô livre des livres, combien d'heures sereines ne te dois-je pas! Lire la Bible, c'est monter au sommet d'une montagne d'où l'on embrasse du même regard toute l'île et l'immensité océane qui la cerne. Alors toutes les petitesses de la vie sont balayées, l'âme déploie ses grandes ailes et plane, ne connaissant plus que des choses sublimes et éternelles. (**167**)

In the first section of Chapter X, and again in the closing pages of the text, the metaphorical mountain is replaced by a real one as Robinson, climbing to the peak of the rocky *chaos,* experiences the *extase solaire.* He has reached the end of his spiritual journey, entering the 'Cité solaire' as predicted in Van Deyssel's tarot reading. Before, the Bible provided the only 'viatique spirituel'; now, the physical island itself fulfils that role.

In *Robinson Crusoe,* the religion which Crusoe discovers is the mainland Christian faith. The role played by the island in his spiritual transformation is largely restricted to its uninhabited status: Crusoe changes before Friday arrives, then sets about transforming Friday in his turn. His new-found faith does initially alter his attitude to the island:

> Now I began to construe the words mentioned above, *Call on me, and I will deliver you,* in a different sense from what I had ever done before; for then I had no notion of any thing being called deliverance, but my being delivered from the captivity I was in; for tho' I was indeed at large in the place, yet the island was certainly a prison to me, and that in the worst sense in the world; but now I learned to take it in another sense. Now I looked back upon my past life with such horrour, and my sins appeared so dreadful, that my soul sought nothing of God but deliverance from the load of guilt that bore down all my comfort... (*RC,* 111)

And yet, in spite of this claim, Crusoe leaves the island at the first opportunity. The natural environment is never an active force; it does not offer up an alternative spirituality or path to salvation, indeed it, like Friday, is changed by Crusoe: the Puritan work ethic is consonant with his westernising endeavours. The process, in other words, is one-way: by the close of the text everything, and everyone, fits into the mainland mould.

In *Vendredi,* Robinson's new-found spiritual sense is intimately bound in with the physical island. Although he initially attempts to transform both it and Vendredi, any changes remain superficial or cosmetic, and the island reverts to its natural state. Vendredi and the island are active forces representing alternatives to the mainland (European, Christian) system. Robinson begins to change in the first half of the text, but his progress is arrested until Vendredi arrives to lead the way towards the *extase solaire.* The 'inner voice' of the Holy Ghost, far from condoning Robinson's contruction projects, seems to urge him to follow the dictates of the *homme nouveau.* Like his predecessor, Tournier's Robinson initially equates salvation with escape: his planned escape vessel, the *Évasion,* is for him a 'navire de salut' (**27**). However, by the closing stages of the text he realises that it is in fact the island environment itself which is to be his salvation:

> Ainsi étais-je amené par tâtonnements successifs à *chercher mon salut* dans la communion avec des éléments, étant devenu moi-même élémentaire. (**226**; my emphasis)

Unlike Defoe's hero, he chooses to remain on the island.

In *Robinson Crusoe,* the spiritual and physical realms remain discrete: as far as Crusoe's religious experiences are concerned, the

physical location is not of paramount importance. In some respects a
prison cell might have served the purpose just as well as a desert island.
In *Vendredi*, the spiritual world which Robinson discovers stems
directly from the physical, natural world; in a sense, it is that world.
Elsewhere in the text we see the spiritual and the sensuous, the sacred
and the sexual, coexist. Robinson's sexual explorations of Speranza form
an integral part of his spiritual development. When he first names the
island, he recalls both the Christian virtue of Hope and a previous sexual
liaison. While he is kneading the dough for his first loaf of bread, he
both recognises the wealth of religious symbolism associated with the
'daily bread' and revels in the sensuous pleasures of touch and smell
(**81**).

In Defoe's novel, the proselytising Crusoe is quick to cover up the
body of the naked Friday, who, typically, accepts these tokens of
Western society as readily as he embraces his new faith: 'I [...] let him
know that I would give him some cloaths, at which he seemed very glad,
for he was stark naked' (*RC*, 209). In *Vendredi*, Robinson's spiritual
transformation goes hand in hand with his physical metamorphosis.
Early in the text he expresses a puritanical disgust towards his own
body; under Vendredi's influence he bathes in the sun's rays (earlier
feared) and learns to exult in his own strength and agility. Inspired by
Vendredi's beauty, he realises that grace—in both the spiritual and the
physical sense—can be united in the human form (**217**). The world of
*Vendredi* might be summed up by the words of another of Tournier's
characters, the seminarist Thomas Koussek in *Les Météores*, who has
trained in the oriental spiritualist tradition:

> En vérité tout est sacré. Vouloir distinguer parmi les choses un domaine
> profane et matériel au-dessus duquel planerait le monde sacré, c'est
> simplement avouer une certaine cécité et en cerner les limites. (*M*, 158)

Robinson begins the text a puritanical Quaker, and ends it standing on a
rocky promontory soaking up the rays of an apparently life-giving sun,
the last of the four natural elements, fire. What are we to make of this?
Does Robinson's new spirituality constitute a wholesale rejection of
Christianity?

The *extase solaire* represents the culminating point of those moments
when Robinson had experienced a sense of harmony and participation
with natural, elemental forces. The first observation we can make is that
the experience of the *extase solaire* reveals several of the traits
associated with religious mysticism. In his work *Mysticism*, F.C.
Happold includes the following characteristics in his description of the
mystical experience: sensations of serenity and joy; heightened
awareness; a sense of timelessness; passivity; the overcoming of dualities
(Happold, 43-8).

Throughout *Vendredi*, as we have seen, the steps in Robinson's spiritual journey have been characterised by feelings of elation (the sensation of being 'en vacances' as early as Chapter II), and self-assurance. During the *extase solaire,* such emotions are expressed typically in the language of paradox and antithesis: 'il faisait face à l'extase solaire avec une joie presque douloureuse' (**254**). The mystic's vision is often marked by an abnormal sharpening of the senses and an awareness of unity and harmony. Standing on the *chaos,* Robinson is acutely aware of every sight and sound; the cry of a seagull, the intense blue of the sky, the flowers themselves. The harmony which typified Robinson's earlier glimpses of natural beauty is all-pervading: 'Les oiseaux et les insectes emplirent l'espace d'un concert unanime' (*ibid.*).

As he awaits the sunrise, Robinson believes that he kneels not before an astral body but a deity, no mere natural phenomenon, as he earlier insists that 'l'Astre Majeur est autre chose qu'une flamme gigantesque, qu'il a de l'esprit en lui, et qu'il a le pouvoir d'irradier d'éternité les êtres qui savent s'ouvrir à lui' (**244**). Whether we accept the supernatural element in the story or not (and we saw in Chapter Two that this remains perfectly ambiguous), the fact remains that in Robinson's mind at least, time has been suspended.

Mysticism is traditionally associated with passivity, reflected in Robinson's desire to lay himself open to the sun's rays: 'je m'ouvre à la fécondation de l'Astre Majeur' (**230**). As we shall see in the next chapter, this passivity is linked to a reversal of gender roles. Up to this point Robinson had cast himself in the (traditionally) active male role, regarding Speranza as the passive bride. Certainly there has been a marked shift away from the aggressive dominance of the *vieil homme;* rather than seeking to force others into a role he has designated (half-caste slave; land to be cultivated and westernised), Robinson has been moving towards a situation in which he can accept both Vendredi and the island on their own terms. Shortly after the first passage describing the *extase solaire,* something of his new state of mind is revealed as he attempts to understand and empathise with the phenomena around him (here, specifically a wild hare) rather than control and impose his own point of view: 'J'essaie de me figurer l'univers de cet animal dont le flair prodigieux joue le rôle prédominant qui revient à la vision chez l'homme' (**223**).

In the course of a mystical experience, dualities may be overcome. Although Robinson casts himself in the role of 'épouse', he believes that the male / female gender categories have become redundant: 'la différence de sexe est dépassée' (**230**). Vendredi represents the deity Venus, whilst the moon, traditionally female, is referred to in male terms: 'le Grand Luminaire Halluciné' (*ibid.*). More significantly, the duality which separates man and God may be dissolved; when Robinson describes himself in terms of a 'statue surhumaine', he seems to share the mystic's belief that man can partake of the divine (**216**). Such a belief is not so distant from the Quaker faith in which he was brought up: Fox himself was accused of heresy when he stated that he was the son of God, and that God dwelled within him. We are certainly a long way from the chasm separating fallen mankind from God in Defoe's *Robinson Crusoe*.

Clearly Robinson's experiences place him outside the orthodox Christian tradition, but if we accept that the *extase solaire* represents a mystical experience, we are still left with the question: is this mysticism to be regarded as a complete rejection of Christianity? Before attempting to answer it, we should look more closely at the two principal passages describing Robinson as he awaits the sunrise on the *chaos*:

> Suspendue au-dessus des dunes du levant, une chapelle ardente rougeoyait où se préparaient mystérieusement les fastes de l'héliophanie. J'ai mis un genou à terre et je me suis recueilli, attentif à la métamorphose de la nausée qui m'habitait en une attente mystique à laquelle participaient les animaux, les plantes et même les pierres. Quand j'ai levé les yeux la chapelle ardente avait éclaté, et c'était maintenant un grand reposoir qui encombrait la moitié du ciel de sa masse ruisselante d'or et de pourpre. Le premier rayon qui a jailli s'est posé sur mes cheveux rouges, telle la main tutélaire et bénissante d'un père. Le second rayon a purifié mes lèvres, comme avait fait jadis un charbon ardent celles du prophète Isaïe. Ensuite deux épées de feu ayant touché mes épaules, je me suis relevé chevalier solaire. Aussitôt une volée de flèches brûlantes ont percé ma face, ma poitrine et mes mains, et la pompe grandiose de mon sacre s'est achevée tandis que mille diadèmes et mille sceptres de lumière couvraient ma statue surhumaine. (**215-16**)

> Robinson avait oublié l'enfant. Redressant sa haute taille, il faisait face à l'extase solaire avec une joie presque douloureuse. Le rayonnement qui l'enveloppait le lavait des souillures mortelles de la journée précédente et de la nuit. Un glaive de feu entrait en lui et transverbérait tout son être. Speranza se dégageait des voiles de la brume, vierge et intacte. En vérité cette longue agonie, ce noir cauchemar n'avaient jamais eu lieu. L'éternité, en reprenant possession de lui, effaçait ce laps de temps sinistre et dérisoire. Une profonde inspiration l'emplit d'un sentiment d'assouvissement total. Sa poitrine se bombait comme un bouclier d'airain. Ses jambes prenaient appui sur le roc, massives et inébranlables comme des colonnes. La lumière fauve le revêtait d'une armure de jeunesse inaltérable et lui forgeait un masque de cuivre d'une régularité implacable où étincelaient des yeux de diamant. Enfin l'astre-dieu déploya tout entière sa couronne de cheveux rouges dans des explosions de cymbales et des stridences de trompettes. Des reflets métalliques s'allumèrent sur la tête de l'enfant.
> —Comment t'appelles-tu? lui demanda Robinson.
> —Je m'appelle Jaan Neljapäev. Je suis né en Estonie, ajouta-t-il comme pour excuser ce nom difficile.
> —Désormais, lui dit Robinson, tu t'appelleras Jeudi. C'est le jour de Jupiter, dieu du Ciel. C'est aussi le dimanche des enfants. (**254**)

At first glance, the *extase solaire* does indeed seem to represent a break with the Christian church. Not only is there no overt mention of a Christian God, but Robinson appears to pray to the sun itself. The neologism 'héliophanie' is employed to describe the sunrise. If a theophany is the manifestation of the divine to man, then here that deity is an astral body. What is more, the era of the *extase solaire* is closely associated with the pagan gods of mythology. Robinson realises that Vendredi's name is linked to the death of Christ (Good Friday) and the birth of Venus, goddess of love (**228**). As predicted by Van Deyssel's Tarot-card reading, Robinson is saved by Jaan, apparently an incarnation of Jupiter, 'dieu du ciel'(**13**).

Yet for all this, it can be argued that Christianity is not eliminated from the text, for aspects of that tradition permeate the two descriptions of the *extase solaire*. When Robinson describes the sunrise, he uses terms usually associated with High Church or Catholic ceremony: the sky is 'une chapelle ardente', a 'reposoir' whose predominant colours are gold and purple. Robinson is pierced by shafts of sunlight as Saint Sebastian was martyred by a shower of arrows: 'une volée de flèches ont percé ma face, ma poitrine et mes mains'(**216**).

In *Le Vent Paraclet*, Tournier deplores the placing of the crucifixion at the centre of orthodox Christian iconography, seeing this as yet another sign of that tradition's rejection of the body:

> L'horreur de la chair place le crucifix—une charogne clouée sur deux poutres—au centre du culte catholique, de préférence à tout autre symbole chrétien, le Christ rayonnant de la Transfiguration par exemple. (*VP*, 65)

The orthodox Church, says Tournier, rejects the body and rejects physical love, but 'la chair aimée et célébrée en ceux que nous aimons resplendit comme celle de Jésus sur le mont Thabor' (*ibid.*). It is precisely this positive image of the physical splendour of Christ on Mount Tabor which is echoed in the two descriptions of Robinson, bathed in sunlight atop the *chaos,* exulting in his physical beauty and strength.

Further Christian imagery can be found in the second description of the *extase solaire*. Robinson's chest is referred to as a 'bouclier d'airain'; the sunlight clothes him in 'une armure de jeunesse', and forges him 'un masque de cuivre'. The imagery of armour echoes the words in Paul's letter to the Ephesians:

> Put on all the armour which God provides, so that you may be able to stand firm against the devices of the devil. [...] Therefore take up God's armour; then you will be able to stand your ground when things are at their worst, to complete every task and still to stand. Stand firm, I say. [...] for coat of mail put on integrity [...] take up the great shield of faith [..]. Take salvation for helmet; for sword, take that which the spirit gives you. (VI: 10-18)

The repeated invocation to 'stand firm' is translated into the description of Robinson's physical stance: 'ses jambes prenaient appui sur le roc, massives et inébranlables comme des colonnes'. In *Robinson Crusoe,* a single faith is represented. In *Vendredi,* the elemental forces of nature, Christian imagery and pagan gods come together in a syncretic vision.

One more crucial point remains to be made. Although we might think that the emphasis on the sun, or the element fire, introduces a purely pagan note into the text, another of Tournier's texts points to an alternative reading. In *Les Météores,* we learn from the character Thomas Koussek that: 'Auparavant, le feu, étant source de lumière et de chaleur, était symbole divin, présence sensible de Dieu, manifestation de l'Esprit-Saint' (*M.,* 150). Robinson started out a Quaker, and he maintains his faith in the Holy Ghost throughout the text. Now, in the final pages of *Vendredi,* the presence of the Holy Ghost returns. Earlier in the text, Robinson had referred to his mother's Quaker beliefs and described her as 'une femme inspirée, au plus haut sens du mot' (**107**). Now, as he soaks up the sun's rays, the same word is employed: 'Une profonde inspiration l'emplit d'un sentiment d'assouvissement total'. At Pentecost the Holy Ghost descended on the apostles in tongues of flame. Here, both Robinson and the young boy Jaan are touched by the flames of the sun: 'le premier rayon qui a jailli s'est posé sur mes cheveux rouges' (**216**); 'des reflets métalliques s'allumèrent sur la tête de l'enfant' (**254**).

We should not be surprised to find such an emphasis on the Holy Ghost in *Vendredi,* for Tournier's interest in the subject is evident. The title of his autobiographical *Le Vent Paraclet* is itself a reference to the third Person of the Trinity (a 'paraclete' is an advocate, comforter or intercessor; the term is used to describe the Holy Ghost: 'Jesus replied [...] your Advocate, the Holy Spirit whom the Father will send in my name, will teach you everything'—*John,* XIV: 26). The character Koussek trained at the 'monastère du Paraclet'. In *Le Vent Paraclet,* Tournier expresses his interest in the twelfth-century biblical scholar Joachim of Fiore, whose ideas add an interesting dimension to our reading of *Vendredi* (*VP,* 261). Joachim believed that two divine Persons, Christ and the Holy Ghost, were sent to man by God. The descent of the Holy Ghost, regarded by Joachim as a divine Person fully equal to the Father and Son, would herald a Third Age or Tertius Status, a new age of peace, harmony, and spiritual insight:

> The first status was under the law, the second status under grace, the third status, which we expect soon, will be under a more ample grace [...]; the first was lived in the servitude of slaves, the second in the servitude of sons, but the third will be in liberty; the first was a time of chastisings, the second of action, but the third will be a time of contemplation; the first was lived in fear, the second in faith, the third will be in love; the first was the

status of slaves, the second of sons, but the third will be that of friends; the first of old men, the second of young men, the third of children. (Reeves, 14)

Before Vendredi's arrival Robinson might be said to have been living in the First Age of the Father and the Law. In the first half of *Vendredi*, Old Testament texts are cited on a number of occasions, and Robinson himself remarks that with his fixed expression and beard he ressembles an Old Testament patriarch: 'C'était bien à l'Ancien Testament et à sa justice sommaire qu'elle [la barbe] ressortissait, ainsi d'ailleurs que ce regard trop franc dont la violence mosaïque effrayait' (**90**). Vendredi, as Christ-figure, heralds the beginning of the Second Age, brought to a close by his death (or departure), opening the way to the Third Age of the Holy Ghost. The conclusion of *Vendredi* reflects many of the characteristics of this Tertius Status: the emphasis is indeed on love, friendship and children, all of which are symbolised by the young boy Jaan.

The arrival of the cabin-boy also introduces a certain tension into the text, the very last words of which record Robinson's words to his young companion. Rather than casting off his human attributes and merging with elemental forces, Robinson seems to 'return' to the world of human relationships. Interestingly, when Tournier wrote *Vendredi*, he originally planned a quite different conclusion to the text: Robinson would remain alone on the island having become a stylite, or religious recluse, standing motionless upon a column of sunlight. The revised ending of the novel highlights the importance of human relations. The presence of the young boy also, as we shall see in the next chapter, reintroduces a note of sexual ambiguity into the text.

# Chapter Four

## Sexual Relations

Cela vous conduit à dire que l'idéal, c'est l'être moyen,
ce qui suppose bêtise, laideur, ignorance et médiocrité.
C'est proprement affreux. Voilà ce que recouvre le mot 'normal'.
On ne le dénoncera jamais assez.

(TOURNIER)

Although the original Robinson Crusoe story may by its very nature have little room for the female sex, many of the *robinsonnades* which have succeeded it also exclude women from their cast of characters. In *Vendredi*, Tournier moves some way from this tradition as he turns his attention to the psychosexual changes undergone by his castaway, reintroducing male / female relations into the myth. Tournier is an author who likes to provoke his readers by challenging and subverting norms, and one of his favourite targets is the heterosexual relationship: 'on pourrait mettre les mariés en garde: "ne réunissez pas ce que Dieu a séparé" ', he has said, in typically provocative mode (Tournier, 1970: 6). In the light of such comments it hardly surprising that Robinson's sex-life follows a rather unusual path.

Sex could hardly be said to rear its ugly head in *Robinson Crusoe*, in fact it seems scarcely to impinge upon the hero's consciousness. The twenty-eight year period of sexual abstinence which Crusoe is obliged to endure elicits only a passing comment. Citing the Gospels, he observes with some satisfaction: 'I was removed from all the wickedness of the world here. I had neither *the lust of the flesh, the lust of the eye*, or *the pride of life*' (*RC*, 139; author's emphasis). The subject is not raised again. Crusoe is a single man when he sets off on his adventures, and when he does marry towards the end of the novel, during a lull in his seafaring adventures, his wife is both introduced into the text and swiftly dispatched within the space of a single sentence:

> In the mean time I in part settled my self here [England]; for first of all I marry'd, and that not either to my disadvantage or dissatisfaction, and had three children, two sons and a daughter: but my wife dying, and my nephew coming home with good success from a voyage to Spain, my inclination to go abroad, and his importunity, prevailed and engaged me to go in his ship, as a private trader to the East Indies. (*RC*, 298)

The only other mention of women as potential partners comes in the closing pages of the novel, when Crusoe reports that he sent the island colonisers seven women 'such as I found proper for service, or for wives to such as would take them'. Eager to see his colony prosper, he generously promises to ship more women from England and other 'necessaries', such as 'five cows, three of them being big with calf, some sheep, and some hogs' (*RC*, 299).

From the opening pages of *Vendredi,* we realise that Tournier's Robinson will not emulate his rather asexual predecessor's indifference to 'the lust of the flesh'. Tournier's protagonist is a married man, and his status as a gendered, presumably heterosexual being is brought to our attention by the enigmatic Captain Van Deyssel's hesitant reproach: 'Vous avez abandonné... euh... laissé à York une jeune épouse et deux enfants' (**8**). Robinson is quick to reveal his interest in (hetero)sexual matters: the new name he selects for the island—Speranza—reminds him of 'une ardente Italienne' whom he had known during his student days (**45**). This first association marks the beginning of an evolving relationship. As the text unfolds, Robinson comes to see Speranza not only as an area of land to be cultivated, but as a female being. When he draws a map of the island it assumes the form of a woman:

> Il lui semblait d'ailleurs, en regardant d'une certaine façon la carte de l'île [...], qu'elle pouvait figurer le profil d'un corps féminin sans tête, une femme, oui, assise, les jambes repliées sous elle, dans une attitude où l'on n'aurait pu démêler ce qu'il y avait de soumission, de peur ou de simple abandon. (**46**)

The image of a headless (brainless?) woman in a position of submission or sexual receptiveness is almost stereotypic in its sexism, and indeed, Tournier's representations of the female sex have given rise to some criticism (see Maclean, 1988). We should note, however, that in this case the description of the decapitated woman is presented very much as Robinson's subjective view of his art-work: these are the perceptions of the *vieil homme,* Robinson-the-coloniser, who seeks to master his environment. The narrator, typically, offers no comment. Seen in this light, the provocative description comes close to the parodic.

Devoid of human company prior to Vendredi's arrival, Robinson comes to consider Speranza as an Other (*autrui*) with whom he can communicate: 'en l'absence de tout autre interlocuteur, il poursuivait avec elle un long, lent et profond dialogue'. The island seems to approve or condemn Robinson's actions: 'ses gestes, ses actes et ses entreprises constituaient autant de questions auxquelles l'île répondait par le bonheur ou l'échec qui les sanctionnaient' (**56**). The apparent reciprocity of the relationship, whereby the island appears to approve or disapprove Robinson's actions, is, however, belied by a hierarchical pattern of domination and submission which prevails throughout the first half of the text. Robinson is intent upon pursuing his 'civilising' course, and consequently pays little heed to, and certainly does not act upon, any signals which Speranza may seem to emit. Though he claims to regard the island as a subject, he does so strictly on his own terms. In his eyes Speranza is an individual only to the extent that it (she) confirms his own status as male master.

The imbalance in the relationship is underscored, as we saw in Chapter Two (*supra,* p. 21), by Robinson's discovery of a footprint, interpreted by him as a sign of his domination and ownership: 'Speranza—comme une de ces vaches à demi sauvages de la prairie argentine, marquées pourtant au fer rouge—portait désormais le sceau de son Seigneur et Maître' (**57**). The comparison is revealing. Simone de Beauvoir, in her examination of male myths which seek to align woman with natural forces, comments on man's desire to possess a woman absolutely: 'Un des rêves du mâle, c'est de "marquer" la femme de manière qu'elle demeure à jamais sienne' (Beauvoir, 271). To the megalomaniac Robinson, the footprint is just such a stamp of authority.

The metaphor of the branded cow marks a shift in Robinson's perception of the island as woman. Up to this point Speranza has been linked indirectly to the female sex: the name reminds him of a previous sexual liaison; the map representing the island resembles the body of a woman. Soon, however, Robinson begins to perceive the island itself as a female body. Sexual and affective needs which were only implicit before are now articulated as the protagonist becomes aware of 'les besoins nouveaux de son cœur et de sa chair' (**102**). The *grotte* is seen a means of access to the female body of the island: 'il se demandait confusément si la grotte était la bouche, l'œil ou quelque autre orifice naturel de ce grand corps' (*ibid.*). Entering the cavern or grotto Robinson strips off his clothes, anoints his body with milk, and assumes an embryonic position in the inner chamber or *alvéole* (**106**). The exact nature of the feminised island is thus clarified: it has become (literally in Robinson's eyes), a Mother-Earth (or Earth Mother).

What are we to make of this? Perhaps before venturing an interpretation we should quite simply acknowledge that the episode, both comical and touching, typifies Tournier's charm as a modern storyteller who can appeal to all ages. To the child this is no more—or less—than a magical adventure. Once again the text hovers around the fantastic: is the *alvéole* really made to measure?:

> L'intérieur était parfaitement poli, mais curieusement tourmenté, comme le fond d'un moule destiné à informer une chose fort complexe. Cette chose, Robinson s'en doutait, c'était son propre corps... (**106**)

Faced with a non-committal narrator the reader is left to decide for him/herself.

The key to a more sophisticated interpretation of Robinson's telluric experience lies with Freud's account of the development of infantile sexuality. Robinson's experience in the *grotte* can be interpreted as part of an unlearning process, a progressive 'dehumanisation' which opens the way to a subsequent re-learning. According to Freud's account, an infant's psychosexual development reaches a crucial stage around the age of three to five years with the onset of the Oedipal complex, a term used to describe and account for the triangular relationship linking the child with his (in this case) father and mother. (Freud takes the name from Sophocles's tragedy of the fifth century B.C., in which the mythological Greek king Oedipus is destined to kill his father and marry his mother.) The male child takes his mother as his primary love-object (the object of both affection and sexual desire), simultaneouly experiencing feelings of great ambivalence towards his father, who is seen as both a threat and a rival. There follows a period of latency in sexual development until the child reaches puberty some nine or ten years later, at which point the problem of object-choice resumes where it had left off. The child ideally resolves the Oedipal complex by detaching his libidinal wishes from his mother, reconciling himself with his father, and finding a love-object similar to, but not identical with, his mother (Freud, 1963: 330-37).

With this somewhat simplified account in mind, we can go some way towards an interpretation of Robinson's relationship with the island-as-mother. The initially beneficial effects of his experience in the *alvéole*—Robinson discovers a deep-seated security (111)—reflect the importance of the unconditional love which binds a child to his mother. The infant's typically incestuous desire (Freud notes that a child's first love-objects—parents and siblings—are always incestuous in nature) is reflected both in the image of the island as mother and in Robinson's thoughts whilst in the *alvéole*, which turn to his real mother and father. The metaphor describing his mother as a 'terre accueillante' is reversed as the 'terre' or island assumes a maternal role (108).

When Robinson realises that Speranza's water supplies have run dry, that his crops are failing and his goats giving birth to dead kids, he concludes that his imposition of a maternal vocation upon the island is misguided. He is not a child but a fully-grown man whose ejaculations in the inner chamber of the cavern threaten to impregnate the 'île-mère' (114). On this occasion, therefore, Robinson does accept and respond to the 'messages' sent out by Speranza. We might see Robinson's decision to bring an end to his ventures into the cave in terms of a resolution of the Oedipal complex: he turns away from the incestuous nature of the relationship with the mother-figure. Interestingly, although the first experience in the *alvéole* was seen by him in a positive light, upon emerging from the 'grotte' he is temporarily blinded by the sun: 'Une douleur fulgurante lui dévora les yeux. Il couvrit son visage de ses mains' (**110**). When the Oedipus of Greek mythology discovers that he has fulfilled his destined fate, he blinds himself by way of punishment. The incest taboo in Robinson's case is thus signalled early on.

Freud points out in his discussion of the Oedipal complex that puberty rites in primitive races often represent a rebirth which has the sense of releasing the initiate from the incestuous bond with his mother, and Robinson's experiences in the *alvéole* can also be regarded in terms of such initiation ceremonies (Freud, 1963: 335). Examining rites in primitive cultures, Mircea Eliade notes that these often take the form of the initiate's entering a hut representing a telluric womb. Initiation ceremonies usually involve physical hardships such as fasting, darkness, and silence — all in evidence here. Entering the hut signifies a return to chaos, to a pre-formal state, a latent mode of being. The initiate's emergence from the hut is perceived as a rebirth, compared to the creation of the world, and thus signifying a new state of being for the initiate (see Eliade, 1975: ix-20). Viewed in this light, Robinson too can be considered as an initiate into a new order. His rebirth from the earth-womb (he emerges naked and in tears, like a newborn infant) marks a stage in his journey away from the Defoe prototype.

Once again the image of the earth-mother typifies those myths analysed (and criticised) by feminist critics such as Beauvoir:

> L'homme recherche dans la femme l'Autre comme Nature and comme son semblable. Mais on sait quels sentiments ambivalents la Nature inspire à l'homme. Il l'exploite mais elle l'écrase, il naît d'elle et il meurt en elle [...] elle est la contingence et l'Idée [...]. Tour à tour alliée, ennemie, elle apparaît comme le chaos ténébreux d'où sourd la vie [...] et comme l'au-delà vers lequel elle tend: la femme résume la nature en tant que Mère, épouse et Idée; ces figures tantôt se confondent et tantôt s'opposent et chacune d'elles a un double visage. (Beauvoir, 243)

Although the myths associated with woman-as-mother most often assume a negative form — man is reminded of his contingency — it is the positive aspect of the myth which we see exemplified in *Vendredi:* 'la femme appartient à la Nature, elle est traversée par le courant infini de la vie; elle apparaît donc comme la médiatrice entre l'individu et le cosmos' (*ibid.*, 284). Robinson's perception of the island as a mother figure clearly reflects that aspect of the myth which values woman as a go-between linking man and nature. Van Deyssel's prophetic words — 'Il s'est retiré au fond d'une grotte pour y retrouver sa source originelle' (8) — echo Beauvoir's delineation of the myth: 'l'homme rêve de se confondre à nouveau avec les ténèbres maternelles pour y retrouver les vraies sources de son être' (Beauvoir, 245).

The Robinson who penetrates the body of Speranza is no longer Robinson-the-coloniser, the *vieil homme*, but the *homme nouveau* who seems to alter his dominating perception of the island when he arrests the passage of time by plugging the water-clock and casting off 'ses attributs de gouverneur-général-administrateur' (**101**). When he decides to acclimatise to the darkness of the *grotte*, the conquering ethos remains to some extent: 'il ne lui restait plus qu'à [...] se plier docilement aux exigences du milieu *qu'il voulait conquérir*' (**102**; my emphasis). However, we can detect a shift from the pattern of dominance and submission seen so far. Whilst in the *grotte*, Robinson appears to renounce a sense of self (he is in an 'état d'*inexistence*'— **106**) as he communes with the forces of nature: 'il ne se sentait nullement séparé de Speranza. Au contraire, il vivait intensément avec elle' (**103**).

And yet, though Robinson seems to move towards an acceptance of the island on its own terms, his tendency to cast Speranza in a female role precludes a true acceptance of natural forces. In *Vendredi*, the pattern described by Beauvoir is reversed: it is not woman who is linked to nature but the natural environment which is attributed female status. If the roles are reversed, however, the outcome is the same. Just as the myths Beauvoir describes reduce the status of women from autonomous subjects to mysterious, mythical types, so Robinson's perception of the island as woman indicates that he is still operating within a human (heterosexual) framework, and thus fails to appreciate, and acknowledge, the island and thus natural or elemental forces, in their own right.

After his experiences deep within Speranza in the alveolus or 'womb' of the island, Robinson resurfaces and next directs his sexual energies to the flora and fauna of the island as he engages in the *voie végétale* (**121**). Filled with wonder as he observes the pollination of flowers by insects, he imagines that he too might participate in such a long-distance insemination by carrying pollen from tree to tree. To this end he selects a suitable tree as his sexual partner:

> Enfin il s'étendit nu sur l'arbre foudroyé dont il serra le tronc dans ses bras, et son sexe s'aventura dans la petite cavité moussue qui s'ouvrait à la jonction des deux branches. (*ibid.*)

As is so often the case with *Vendredi*, the episode, which manages to be both provocative and highly amusing—not least because the chosen 'partner' is dead ('foudroyé')—lends itself to more than one level of interpretation. The castaway's motives for pursuing his unusual course of action are far from unambiguous. Has his observation of insect-life really triggered an altruistic desire to help pollinate the trees? Robinson reveals a comical degree of self-delusion when he shifts the responsibility for his actions to the plants themselves. Apparently it is not he who chooses to act in this way but the trees themselves!: 'certains arbres de l'île pourraient s'aviser de l'utiliser [...] pour véhiculer leur pollen' (**120**). Quite apart from the fact that pollination is more than somewhat unlikely to result from his arboreal probings, Robinson makes no attempt to move from one tree to another: sexual gratification, rather than a selfless desire to carry pollen, seems to win the day...

Like the descent into the *grotte,* this episode is open to a more serious level of interpretation. Robinson's entry into the *voie végétale* is associated with his perception of the altered state of his sexual desire. Although the desire remains, it is—so he says—no longer directed at women in particular:

> Je sens toujours murmurer en moi cette fontaine de vie, mais elle est devenue totalement disponible. Au lieu de s'engager docilement dans le lit préparé à l'avance par la société, elle déborde de tous les côtés et ruisselle en étoile, cherchant comme à tâtons une voie, la bonne voie où elle se rassemblera et roulera unanime vers un objet. (**119**)

Freud, describing the libido or instinctual sexual drive, notes that it can be considered in terms of four factors: the *source* of excitation, which is internal and organic, the *object,* in other words the person or thing in reality required to satisfy the *aim,* which is to achieve pleasure by removing the *pressure* of excitation. Acquiring a specific aim and object, Freud suggests, requires experience and is a learned process for the newborn infant. Robinson has, apparently, returned to a psychosexual stage prior to the learning of a specific object of desire, and prior also to the Oedipal phase which we suggested was represented by the telluric incident in the *alvéole.*

This unlearning of the 'normal' object of desire—a woman—appears to mark a step in Robinson's progressive dehumanisation, and a shift away from the heterosexual norm. Sex is no longer perceived as something linked to the female body and the 'norm' of procreation—'la perpétuation de l'espèce' (**118**). Robinson goes so far as to consider himself 'le dernier être de la lignée humaine appelé à un retour aux sources végétales de la vie' (**121**). However, though he claims to have forgotten the very concept of woman, the tree is still described in female terms: he dreams of 'les branches de ces arbres [qui] se métamorphoseraient en femmes lascives et parfumées dont les corps incurvés seraient prêts à l'accueillir'. The fallen tree assumes the form of an invitingly recumbent woman with 'deux énormes cuisses noires' (*ibid.*). The ostensibly altruistic desire to participate in the realm of plant life is further undermined by the fact that Robinson's first thoughts when he sees the pollinating insects at work turn to his wife:

> Il se prenait à rêver de quelque oiseau fantastique qui s'enduirait de la semence du Gouverneur de Speranza et volerait jusqu'à York féconder sa femme esseulée. (120)

Evidently his mind is still very much on heterosexual relations.

The description of Robinson's supine sexual partner again centres on a fragmented female body: the tree is regarded as a convenient orifice, as was the *grotte*. Although we might be tempted to perceive this as another example of a certain misogyny, the humour of the incident should not be under-emphasised. Tournier appears not so much to denigrate the female sex, as to parody heterosexual relations and male desire. Although Robinson's attempt to conjure up the vision of a woman focuses on submissiveness and receptiveness to male desire, the sheer excess (and indeed desperation) of his attempts to conjure up the female form surely topples over into the parodic: 'Je prononce: femme, seins, cuisses, cuisses écartelées par mon désir. Rien' (118). Male desire is treated with some parodic distance: Robinson, described circling the chosen tree 'avec des airs louches', takes on all the characteristics of an embarrassed client in a red-light district (122). The narrator's deadpan statement and attribution of a proper name to the tree (of the species *quillai*)—'Il connut de longs mois de liaison heureuse avec Quillai' (121-2)—strikes another light-hearted note, mocking Robinson's attempts to replicate heterosexual relations.

The final sting in the tail comes when Robinson's sexual adventures are brought to a painful conclusion by a spider: 'La douleur ne se calma que plusieurs heures plus tard, cependant que le membre blessé prenait l'aspect d'une mandarine' (122). Earlier, Robinson had admired the sexual display of plants—'la fleur est le sexe de la plante. La plante naïvement offre son sexe à tout venant' and had imagined a new breed of (wo)men 'où chacun porterait fièrement sur sa tête ses attributs mâles ou femelles—énormes, enluminés, odorants...' (121). Comical in its own right, Robinson's desire to break down the boundaries between human and vegetal realms seems all the funnier when we realise that his vegetal dreams almost come true—though a swollen penis resembling a mandarin orange may not have been quite what he had in mind! Once again, the island appears to have communicated its disapproval. Robinson, whose ascetic background makes itself felt, interprets the incident in a moral light—the spider sting represents a form of venereal disease—and retires hurt, abandoning the *voie végétale*.

In spite of his moral misgivings, however, Robinson continues to find outlets for his sexual desire. Speranza assumes the role of 'île-épouse' as the character's sexual advances are directed to the ground itself in the *combe:*

> Il sentait, comme jamais encore, qu'il était couché sur l'île, comme sur
> quelqu'un, qu'il avait le corps de l'île sous lui. [...] La présence presque
> charnelle de l'île contre lui le réchauffait, l'émouvait. Elle était nue, cette
> terre qui l'enveloppait. Il se mit nu lui-même. (**126**)

Robinson provides his own interpretation of the incident in the log-book
entries which follow. His coupling with the island (if 'coupling' is an
apposite term) represents (in his eyes) a further move away from
human models of sexuality towards a pre-social and wholly 'natural'
communion with the earth itself. The earth is closely linked to both
'l'amour' and 'la mort'. The heterosexual act is associated with
procreation, which ultimately signals the annihilation of the individual:
'procréer, c'est susciter la génération suivante qui innocemment, mais
inexorablement, repousse la précédente vers le néant'. As dead bodies
are buried in the ground, Robinson claims that by having sex directly
with Speranza he is simply establishing contact with the earth directly,
missing out the intermediate stage of heterosexual sex (**131**). His act is
thus seen as a fulfilment of 'la vocation géotropique du sexe'. The
deviation from social and human sexual 'norms' brings him in touch
with the elemental forces of nature: 'pour la première fois dans la
combe rose, mon sexe a retrouvé son élément originel, la terre' (**133**).

   This, however, is Robinson's own interpretation of events, and as
such should not necessarily be accepted uncritically. Some aspects of his
analysis make sense. The procreative act may well be seen in terms of
the sacrifice of the individual to ensure the perpetuation of the species,
the supreme biological value. Equally, Robinson's suggestion that human
beings instinctively search out death may be assimilated to Freud's
analysis of the death 'instinct' (*Trieb*), a drive towards the restoration of
an earlier state of things, an 'instinct' which drives the organic entity
back to an inorganic or inanimate state (Freud, 1984: 308-309).
However, Robinson's claim that the sexual act is itself a manifestation of
the death 'instinct' is less easily upheld.

   One aspect of the *combe rose* episode which might support
Robinson's argument that he is making contact with elemental forces is
the growth of the mandrakes. By (apparently) inseminating the earth,
Robinson fathers the mandrakes ('ses filles'), thereby escaping the
inexorable movement towards death signalled by a following human
generation. His dehumanisation, his move away from human models of
sexuality, would seem to be confirmed by the mingling of human and
vegetal realms. The plant progeny would appear to confirm a return to
the 'élément originel' of the earth. However, as we saw in Chapter Two,
a perfect ambiguity surrounds this episode, which may be regarded as
no more than the delusions of the protagonist.

   Whichever way we decide to interpret the mandrake episode, we can
see that in spite of Robinson's claims to have departed from the

heterosexual norm, the *combe rose* episode, like the *voie végétale* before it, maintains the male / female gender roles. The word *combe*, for example, is linked linguistically (and humorously) by Robinson to the female anatomy: 'Combe... combe... Il voyait un dos de femme un peu gras, mais d'un port majestueux [...]. Les LOMBES!' (**127**). Robinson's previous (hetero)sexual relationships are clearly not totally forgotten. Rather than an inhuman communion with the element earth, the sexual act is still described in terms of a relationship between male and female partners. Speranza apparently responds to Robinson's own sexuality:

> Son visage fermé fouillait l'herbe jusqu'aux racines, et il souffla de la bouche une haleine chaude en plein humus. Et la terre répondit, elle lui renvoya au visage une bouffée surchargée d'odeurs qui mariait l'âme des plantes trépassées et le remugle poisseux des semences, des bourgeons en gestation. (**126**)

After the event, he even goes so far as to endow Speranza with powers of speech, interpreting the biblical words in the 'Song of Songs' as those of the island: 'et Speranza lui répondait [...] *'Je suis à mon bien-aimé et mon bien-aimé est à moi / il fait paître son troupeau parmi mes lis'* (**135**), though misquoting: the original line reads 'parmi les lis'.

Gender stereotypes still operate: Robinson is very much the active male, whilst the island is typically represented as fecund and passive. Beauvoir draws an analogy between the sexual act and man's desire to conquer new (preferably virgin) lands:

> Il veut conquérir, prendre, posséder; avoir une femme, c'est la vaincre; il pénètre en elle comme le soc dans les sillons; il la fait sienne comme il fait sienne la terre qu'il travaille; il laboure, il plante, il sème. (Beauvoir, 256)

The image of the active male and the ploughing metaphor is echoed in Robinson's sexual act, though it is perhaps tempered by a sense of communion: 'Son sexe creusa le sol comme un soc et s'y épancha dans une immense pitié pour toutes choses créées' (**126**). Just as Robinson claimed to act from altruistic motives by pollinating the trees, so it is now suggested that he acts selflessly in satisfying the island: 'à apaiser en elle son angoisse et désir' (**136**). Once more we can detect a process of rationalisation at work. Shortly after the *combe rose* incident, Robinson once again assumes the dominant role and Speranza is seen as the submissive bride: 'Or ce matin-là avait une splendeur nuptiale, et Speranza était prosternée à ses pieds' (**134**). Vendredi, some ten pages later, will find himself in a similar position.

Tensions or ambiguities are maintained throughout Robinson's various 'relationships' with the island. On the one hand, we may be tempted to interpret his activities as no more than the products of his (very natural) sexual frustrations. In spite of his altruistic claims and suggestions that he is making contact with natural, elemental forces, his sophisticated (and often sophistic) arguments—for example, his suggestion that the sexual act and the earth are linked because lovers are habitually drawn to a prone position on the ground—could be dismissed as no more than deluded rationalisations. Even if we do accept that a process of dehumanisation is taking place (and the Freudian echoes in the text certainly invite this level of interpretation), we should realise that although Robinson seems at times to commune more closely with Speranza, human gender roles and sexual stereotypes are for the most part maintained. Casting the island in a female role enables Robinson to assert his identity as dominant male.

As might be expected, Vendredi's arrival in the second half of the text leads to a shift in Robinson's sexual relations with the island. It is now Vendredi who serves to reinforce Robinson's status as dominant subject. Initially, the *vieil homme* re-emerges: as Robinson seeks to fit Vendredi into his westernised system, 'l'île administrée' takes precedence over the 'île-épouse'. Tensions, however, remain. Robinson has come too far to reassume the role of dominant coloniser: the *homme nouveau* struggles with the Defoe prototype, prompting Robinson to push Vendredi to the limits in a desire to precipitate a crisis.

This crisis, in fact, centres on Robinson's sexual relations with the island. When he discovers the striped mandrakes in the *combe rose* (**166**), then catches Vendredi *in flagrante delicto* with Speranza (**176**), his disquiet turns to jealous rage as his absolute possession of his female partner is threatened. As well as a representing a reflection of the Western myth of the potency of the black man, the incident, depicting a 'love triangle', can once again be read as a parodic gibe at heterosexual relations. The episode also marks a stereotypical reaction to infidelity, whereby the fickle woman is ultimately held responsible: the biblical passage read by Robinson (*'Tu t'es étendue comme une courtisane'*— **178**) is interpreted by him as a sign of Speranza's 'seduction' of the innocent male victim, Vendredi.

The act of betrayal apparently leads to a real shift in Robinson's relationship with the island. After the explosion, Speranza is no longer perceived in human (female) terms. Vendredi is to herald the beginning of a new, more truly elemental communion with natural forces. Robinson realises that:

> ... l'ère de l'île épouse—qui succédait à l'île mère, elle-même postérieure à l'île administrée—vient à son tour de prendre fin, et que le temps est proche de l'avènement de choses absolument nouvelles, inouïes et imprévisibles. (**180**)

If Robinson no longer looks to Speranza to confirm his own maleness, it is because his sexuality is no longer gender-specific. Robinson himself comments on this shift away from gendered, genital sexuality in the extended log-book entry of Chapter X. Here, he confirms what the reader should already have noted: hitherto, his 'amours avec Speranza s'inspiraient encore fortement des modèles humains' (**229**). Now, he states, his sexuality has moved away not only from heterosexual relations, but from any human model of sexuality. If he is not tempted to engage in a homosexual relationship with Vendredi, it is because such human notions of sexuality have been superseded by a fusion with the elements. The 'volupté brutale'—the orgasm of human sex—associated with a diminution of vital forces ('une perte de substance qui laisse l'animal triste *post coitum'* — **230**), has been replaced by a 'jubilation douce' which unites Robinson with the elemental forces of the sun and sky. Although he is reluctant to employ anthropomorphic terms, claiming that all differentiation between the sexes has become redundant, when he does it is to invert the pattern so far and cast himself in a passive, female role: 'c'est sous les espèces féminines, et comme l'épouse du ciel qu'il conviendrait de me définir' (*ibid.*). This, Robinson claims, marks the fulfilment of Van Deyssel's prophecy: he has attained the perfection of a 'sexualité circulaire' which transcends gender distinctions.

But has Robinson really gone beyond human models of sexuality? The analysis, after all, is strictly limited to the log-book, and as such does not necessarily represent a reliable point of view. Ever provocative, Tournier plants a seed of doubt in our minds by introducing the young boy Jaan into the text. In Chapter Six, I will suggest that the ending of *Vendredi* invites speculation. The reader projects into an imaginary future: what does the future hold for Robinson and his young companion?

For the reader who is familiar with Tournier's other writings, the nature of the relationship between the two male characters remains deeply ambiguous. On the one hand we are invited to consider this as a paternal relationship based on an affective bond. Jaan, who has red hair and a fair complexion like Robinson, may be seen to asume a purely filial role. Certain factors suggest that by introducing the boy into the text Tournier may be underlining the need for human warmth and physical affection.

Overcome by despair, Robinson finds a page torn from the Bible. A passage from the first book of *Kings* describes how King David was kept warm by a young virgin. Although the passage in *Vendredi* is truncated, the Bible explicitly states that the relationship was not of a sexual nature: 'She was a very beautiful girl, and she took care of the king and waited on him, but he had no intercourse with her' (*Kings I*, 1:

1-3). Elsewhere Tournier has decried the 'tabou physique' which prevails in Western society, pointing especially to the affective deprivation suffered by children in a society which remains 'farouchement antiphysique, mutilante et castratrice' (*VP*, 28). Tournier argues that our primary drive is of an affective rather than a sexual nature. The child's need for physical contact is paramount, and such physicality should not be understood in terms of sexuality alone:

> Quand je parle de contacts physiques, j'entends bien entendu quelque chose de plus vaste et de plus primitif que les jeux érotiques et les relations sexuelles qui n'en sont qu'un cas particulier. (*ibid.*, p. 27)

Bearing such remarks in mind, we can interpret the ending of *Vendredi*, and the relationship between Robinson and Jaan, as one which does no more (or less) than underline human affective needs.

And yet the fact remains that in some of Tournier's other works young boys are explicitly associated with homoerotic desire. In 'Aventures africaines', for instance, one of the stories in *Le Médianoche amoureux* (1989), the narrator of the tale describes how a father seeking a European protector for his son sends the young Arab boy to the narrator's bed. In this case the relationship is clearly of a sexual nature. We saw in the previous chapter that Tournier had originally planned a different ending for *Vendredi*, leaving Robinson alone on the island. Interestingly, one of the characters in *Les Météores*, the gay Alexandre Surin, states that solitude would be bearable were it not for sexual desire:

> Moi, sans sexe, je ne vois vraiment pas de qui j'aurais pu avoir besoin. Un anachorète dans le désert, un stylite debout jour et nuit sur sa colonne. Le sexe, c'est la force centrifuge qui vous chasse dehors. (*M,* 85)

This statement, which echoes the terms of the alternative conclusion to *Vendredi*, might lead us to envisage a quite different relationship between Robinson and Jaan.

Whichever way we consider the end of *Vendredi*—and there is no doubt that our interpretation is coloured by a knowledge of Tournier's other works—the text constitutes a strong challenge to the norm of heterosexuality. Robinson has either escaped from the categorisation of gender and the destructive elements which he perceives to be inseparable from a heterosexual relationship, or finds comfort (whether sexual or not) in the physical presence of the boy Jaan. *Vendredi* seeks to promote our acceptance of all forms of both sexual and physical contact. Ironically, however, the text opens some doors whilst closing others, ending as it does by establishing a scenario which prevails throughout Defoe's *Robinson Crusoe:* the elimination of the female sex.

# Chapter Five

## Seeing Things differently

C'est très difficile de rester un homme
quand personne n'est là pour vous y aider!

(TOURNIER)

In our society, isolation tends to be regarded as a form of punishment. The prisoner is remanded in solitary confinement, the child 'sent to Coventry' or exiled to the bedroom. Most of us spend surprisingly little time on our own, at least in the sense of being completely removed from anything, or anyone, which might provide us with a 'human scale', such as television, or radio. Those who do, popular mythology would have us believe, soon resort to eccentricity: talking to oneself (or to the potted plants) is, after all, said to be the first sign of madness... Given that in Robinson Crusoe's case the exclusion from human society extends to a period of years, even decades, it would be surprising if he did not experience acute psychological difficulties. Tournier, exploring the repercussions of isolation in considerably greater depth than Defoe, shows us a man facing, then striving to overcome, insanity. Ironically, when Robinson's solitude is broken by Vendredi's arrival, the castaway's problems are far from being resolved. The presence of another human being may safeguard the individual against madness, but it can also challenge and threaten him. *Autrui* can at times be something of a necessary evil.

We are left in no doubt that Defoe's Crusoe suffers greatly from his removal from human society; indeed his mental anguish is conveyed in powerful, often extremely poignant language. Despair can strike suddenly, grief inducing an almost catatonic state:

> Before, as I walked about, [...] the anguish of my soul at my condition would break out upon me on a sudden, and my very heart would die within me, to think of the woods, the mountains, the desarts I was in [...]. In the midst of the greatest composures of my mind, this would break out upon me like a storm, and make me wring my hands and weep like a child. Sometimes it would take me in the middle of my work, and I would immediately sit down and sigh, and look upon the ground for an hour or two together; and this was still worse to me; for if I could burst out into tears, or vent my self by words, it would go off, and the grief having exhausted itself would abate. (*RC*, 125)

And yet Crusoe's despair is never more than despair: at no point does he truly peer into the abyss of madness. 'Before'—that is, prior to his discovery of faith—there are moments when he struggles against the miseries of his solitude, work proving in itself to be an effective remedy. Once that religious faith is kindled, Crusoe can give thanks to God 'that He could fully make up to me the deficiencies of my solitary state, and the want of humane society, by His presence and the communications of His grace to my soul' (*RC*, 125). Although Defoe's account of Crusoe's solitude can be moving, the relative ease with which the castaway maintains his mental equilibrium gives rise to a degree of scepticism. In contrast, Tournier's representation of the castaway's plight, of a man whose mental world begins to fall apart, strikes a greater note of realism.

Robinson spends the first period of his isolation expecting company at any moment. Stubbornly refusing to engage in any positive course of action he passes his days (or weeks, months—no record is kept) scrutinising the sea. Eventually this inactivity precipitates the first of a series of crises, as under his fascinated gaze the stretch of ocean begins to assume an alarming form: 'Il vit en elle une surface dure et élastique où il n'aurait tenu qu'à lui de s'élancer et de rebondir'. The hallucinatory experience intensifies, the sea resembles the back of some fantastic creature, the island itself becomes the eyelid and eyebrow of a gigantic eye (**23**). Robinson, glimpsing the shadow of insanity, is afraid. This episode marks the beginning of the erosion of Robinson's normal relations with the objects which surround him. Although equilibrium is temporarily restored as he busies himself with the construction of the *Évasion*, as soon as this project is brought to an untimely end despair overwhelms him, and he retreats into the muddy refuge of the *souille*.

The contrast between Tournier's version of the failed launch and Defoe's handling of a similar event is striking. Tournier highlights the fact that emotions are fuelled and intensified by isolation: the solitary individual easily falls into a state of overwhelming despair. In *Robinson Crusoe*, the hero's inability to shift the boat he has constructed is recounted with a rather phlegmatic detachment. Rather than pointing to Crusoe's vulnerability, the episode is used to convey a sermonising warning to the reader:

> This grieved me heartily, and now I saw, tho' too late, the folly of beginning a work before we count the cost, and before we judge rightly of our strength to go through with it. (*RC*, 139)

Retreat into the *souille* is Robinson's first coping strategy. Faced with an untenable reality, he shuts out or denies that reality, wallowing (literally) in the past. The objective world is rejected in favour of a subjective realm of memory and introspection. The respite proves to be short-lived. Soon Robinson is not merely seeing things differently, but seeing things *tout court*. When a second, more powerful hallucinatory experience (the galleon episode of Chapter II) nearly costs him his life, a new strategy is called for: Robinson will immerse himself not in the mire of the *souille,* but in work. Getting a grip on reality will from now on mean controlling and imposing his will upon his environment. By Chapter III, Robinson has a lucid grasp of the situation and is able to articulate what he perceives to be the root cause of his problems:

> Contre l'illusion d'optique, le mirage, l'hallucination, le rêve éveillé, le fantasme, le délire, le trouble de l'audition... le rempart le plus sûr, c'est notre frère, notre voisin, notre ami ou notre ennemi, mais quelqu'un, grands dieux, quelqu'un! (**55**)

Normality, objective reality, is ultimately a product of consensual opinion. We have all had the experience of turning to another individual in search of confirmation or refutation of our perceptions, our way of seeing: 'is it just me, or is that a... ?'. Robinson does not have that option open to him. In the absence of *autrui* he can no longer trust his own senses, he cannot differentiate between objective reality (what is really 'out there') and his distorted and distorting subjective impressions. Things threaten to get out of perspective, and there is no one there to restore the balance.

Robinson's experiences of psychological disturbance have up to this point in the discussion been described in very unspecific terms. He suffers from hallucinations, and in the face of a potential dissolution of the barrier separating objective reality from subjective impression, sets about establishing a rigorous and ordered system. This level of interpretation is perfectly adequate, but another level can be envisaged. *Vendredi* not only invites comparison with Defoe's *Robinson Crusoe,* it also engages with a current of twentieth-century philosophical thought, specifically with the work of Sartre. More particularly, Robinson's reactions to his isolation can be considered in the light of Sartre's first novel, *La Nausée* (1938).

Like Robinson, Roquentin, the first-person narrator of *La Nausée,* is a solitary individual. Although he is not physically cut off from society, he has no close relationships, and his work as a biographer is such that he spends much of his time alone. As the text opens we see him in a state of crisis. Things are not what they used to be. The objects which surround him assume a threatening and alarming form. Normally we consider the material world in some sort of relation to a human framework. We make sense of objects by naming and categorising them, seeing them in terms of their functions. For Roquentin, these comforting strategies are no longer viable. Objects seem to exist quite gratuitously, free of their labels and functions. He glimpses the contingency, the 'brute existence', the 'thingness' of objects with a visceral immediacy which both sickens and terrifies him.

There are distinct echoes of Roquentin's experiences in *Vendredi*. Robinson's hallucinatory vision of the sea as monster finds a parallel in *La Nausée*. As Roquentin stares into the water, he is overcome with fear and disgust:

> La *vraie* mer est froide et noire, pleine de bêtes; elle rampe sous cette mince pellicule verte qui est faite pour tromper les gens. (Sartre, 175)

Gazing in horrified fascination at the root of a chestnut tree, Roquentin feels its existence escape his attempts to categorise, describe and attribute function:

> J'avais beau répéter: 'C'est une racine'—ça ne prenait plus. Je voyais bien qu'on ne pouvait pas passer de sa fonction de racine, de pompe aspirante, *à ça*, à cette peau dure et compacte de phoque, à cet aspect huileux, calleux, entêté. (*ibid.*, 182)

As Robinson stares at the sea he experiences a similar disjunction between rational knowledge and subjective impression. Although he can articulate a definition of the sea, although he knows 'qu'il n'avait à ses pieds qu'une masse liquide en perpétuel mouvement', the water somehow escapes such a comforting, but reductive, formulation (**22**).

Roquentin's horrified awareness of contingency manifests itself as a gut reaction, a visceral response of nausea ('écœurement') and fear ('angoisse'), feelings which are also experienced by Robinson. Disturbed by the sound of sawing, he tracks down two crabs detaching coconuts from a tree with their pincers, and is sickened: 'Ce spectacle inspira à Robinson un profond dégoût' (**34**). On several occasions the natural world seems threatening and alien, radically Other, and quite separate from Robinson's own existence. When a sea creature directs a jet of water into his face he is momentarily overcome by anxiety: 'la vieille angoisse bien connue et si redoutée lui mordit le foie' (**48**).

The parallels between *Vendredi* and *La Nausée* encourage us to consider Robinson's reactions to his solitude and his activities during the period of the *île administrée* in a different light. So far, his system-building has been seen primarily as a colonial-style, westernising enterprise. But Robinson's careful labelling and categorising of the natural phenomena around him can also be seen as attempts to re-establish or reimpose a human scale, to reduce the threat of contingency. In *La Nausée*, brute existence is described in terms of organic matter, viscosity, and dissolution. Similar terms can be found in Robinson's log-book:

> Je n'aurai de cesse que cette île opaque, impénétrable, pleine de sourdes fermentations et de remous maléfiques, ne soit métamorphosée en une construction abstraite, transparente, intelligible jusqu'à l'os! (**67**)

In the Charter of Chapter IV, Robinson once again seeks to tame the threatening autonomy of the objects around him: 'Scolie: *Toute augmentation de la pression de l'événement brut doit être compensée par un renforcement correspondant de l'étiquette'* (**78**).

*Vendredi*'s engagement with twentieth-century philosophical thought has important repercussions for our reading. Up to this point in this study I have, to some extent, been playing devil's advocate, emphasising those aspects of the text which potentially provoke a hostile response towards Robinson (his self-delusions and cravings for power, his westernising ideals, the transformation of Speranza). This, however, is only half of the picture. Already, by the very act of emphasising the traumas of solitude, Tournier presents Robinson as a potentially more sympathetic character than his predecessor in *Robinson Crusoe,* whose heroic struggles and endeavours threaten at times to alienate (and exasperate) the modern reader. In effect, Tournier's text pulls us in two directions. On the one hand we are reading a work which, by taking Defoe's novel to parodic extremes in its first half, then inverting it in the second, clearly invites us to condemn the Western ethnocentrism of its principal character. At the same time, however, as we filter our response through a contemporary framework, we are tempted into a degree of complicity with Robinson. Here is a man whose fears are not just those of the eighteenth-century coloniser, but of modern man. Robinson's projects may well be exaggerated, but we are led to ask ourselves: would we act any differently? Be he hero, villain or contemporary Everyman, our responses to the castaway are at best (or worst) deeply ambivalent.

Throughout the period of the *île administrée,* Robinson persists with his rigorous categorising and surveying. If the first strategy he employed against insanity was to deny objective reality in the *souille,* the second is to try as far as possible to block off any potentially threatening subjective impressions of the outside world. Objectivity is now all, and reality is consequently counted, labelled, ordered and measured out. But for all this, there are moments, as we saw in Chapter Three, when a new vision of the island emerges, times when far from being threatened by the natural world, Robinson feels a profound sense of harmony with it. A key moment comes when he stops the water-clock and experiences what he is to call his first 'moment d'innocence'.

At the simplest level of interpretation, Robinson experiences a moment of intense happiness and tranquillity. Suddenly seeing things as if with new eyes, he is lost in wonder:

> On aurait dit que cessant soudain de s'incliner les unes vers les autres dans
> le sens de leur usage—et de leur usure—les choses étaient retombées
> chacune de son essence, épanouissaient tous leurs attributs, existaient pour
> elles-mêmes, naïvement, sans chercher d'autre justification que leur propre
> perfection. (**94**)

Moments such as this were earlier described as part of a spiritual
journey, and indeed at this point two strands of thought intersect, for
these episodes can also be considered within the Sartrean framework.
Here Robinson sees the 'brute existence' of things, he is aware of their
contingency ('les choses [...] existaient pour elles-mêmes [...] sans
chercher d'autre justification'), but whereas this way of seeing alarms
and sickens Roquentin, it induces in Robinson a state of 'indicible
allégresse' (**94**). Reality is unveiled just as it is for Sartre's protagonist,
but in Robinson's case the shedding of the wrapping of categories,
functions, definitions and names is a positive moment. His uncovering is
also a discovering: 'Robinson crut découvrir *une autre île*' (*ibid.*). He
sees with the eyes of the mystic, the poet, or—and this is something we
will come back to—the child.

In the extended log-book entry which follows on from this episode,
Robinson dons his philosopher's cap and launches into a lengthy
discourse on 'l'antique problème de la connaissance' (**95**). Existing
debates, he states, have failed to articulate the problem satisfactorily
because they have all been premissed on the existence of *autrui* (**95-6**).
Seeking to remedy the situation, Robinson draws a distinction between
two modes of knowledge or perception and, correlatively, two
conceptions of the Self or Subject.

The first of these, 'l'état primaire de la connaissance', which he states
is 'notre mode d'existence ordinaire' (**97**) can be summed up as follows:
as the seeing subject (which for the sake of linguistic economy I shall
assume to be male) looks upon the world, he is aware only of external
phenomena. He sees (or indeed hears, smells, touches), but is not aware
of himself-seeing. In other words, the self is not at that moment an
object of his consciousness. In this mode, as you read these words, you
are aware of the words and indeed their meaning, but you are not
actively projecting a reading-self, you are not saying to yourself 'I am
reading this text'. Thus Robinson can state: 'Alors Robinson *est*
Speranza. Il n'a conscience de lui-même qu'à travers les frondaisons de
myrtes où le soleil darde une poignée de flèches...' (**98**). Seeing in this
way, according to Robinson, involves a dissolution of the sense of self.
In fact, 'object' and 'subject', self and other, become redundant
categories: there 'is' only the (outside) world. This, for Robinson, is a
purer mode of knowing, one which preserves the 'virginité des choses',
and thus one to which he aspires, imagining an ideal state in which
'chaque chose serait connue, sans personne qui connaisse, consciente,

sans que personne ait conscience...' (**100**). This, however, is possible only in the absence of *autrui*, and correlatively, the absence of self.

Sustaining this mode of perception is difficult. Suddenly a 'déclic' will take place and the purity of vision is shattered as 'le sujet s'arrache à l'objet' (**98**). Now the seeing subject is aware of himself-seeing. As the awareness of the self as seeing subject returns, so the categories of subject and object are once more applicable, 'me' and 'the world out there' are once more distinct. (Returning to the previous analogy, you, as reader, are conscious of yourself-reading the text.)

Once again this section of *Vendredi* draws on Sartrean ideas, though Robinson's views diverge from Sartre's on one important point. Whilst Sartre would agree that a distinction can be drawn between two modes of knowledge, and two conceptions of the self, he would not, as Robinson does, accept that the categories of subject and object can be dispensed with. Sartre too distinguishes between the sense of self we have when we reflect upon our own perceptual acts—what he terms the reflective ego, which might be formulated grammatically as, say, 'j'ai conscience de l'île'—and the pre-reflective ego, the self who sees but does not consciously reflect upon the act of seeing—'il y a conscience de l'île'. Sartre insists, however, that at some level the subject is always aware of the distinction or gap separating himself as subject from the outside world. There can be no knowledge of the world without a knowing subject (and indeed, no knowledge of the self without knowledge of the world).

From the shutting out of the objective world in the *souille* to the shutting out of subjective impression in *l'île administrée*, Robinson has progressed to a way of seeing which presupposes the abolition of the very categories of subjective and objective. By claiming that he has attained such a mode of knowledge, Robinson is turning his back on the rationalist tradition. His is a mystical, intuitive experience. It is also an extra-linguistic one. If there is no consciousness of self, then there can be no articulation of experience (there is no 'I' to articulate it). Moments such as these can only be lived, their effects described retrospectively. Although Robinson does not explicitly link his log-book discussion to his 'moment d'innocence', it does seem that the former is an attempt to describe the latter. Later in this chapter it will be suggested that for all his talk of a breakdown in the subject / object or self / other boundaries, Robinson does, in fact, arrive at a less extreme position by the close of the text.

Although Robinson aspires to the purity of vision associated with *l'autre île*, he cannot sustain it. For the greater part of the text up to Vendredi's arrival, the world of *l'île administrée*, with its labelling and system-building, prevails. Far from losing his sense of self, he asserts his personal identity in various guises. In each case the way in which he sees himself is a function of the way in which he sees the island. Inasmuch as Speranza is (in his eyes) a plot of land to be cultivated, Robinson is a farmer; drawing up the Charter, he is an administrator; where the island is female and submissive, he is, as we have seen, male and dominant. To the extent that the island is a growing replica of the Western society he has left behind, Robinson is (sees himself as) the *Gouverneur* of an imaginary community (the Penal Code and Charter are directed at 'les habitants de l'île'). As long as Robinson projects imaginary others or views the island itself as *autrui,* however, there can be no challenge to his way of seeing things. Once Vendredi arrives, the situation is poised to change.

For all that his religion alleviates the distress of isolation, Defoe's Crusoe finds his desire for human company rekindled when, in the twenty-fourth year of his stay, a ship is wrecked close by the island, with no survivors: ' "O that there had been but one or two; nay, or but one soul saved out of this ship, to have escaped to me, that I might have had one companion, one fellow-creature to have spoken to me [...] !" ' (*RC,* 192). Although his motives may be mixed, when he saves Friday's life it is a deliberate gesture:

> It came now very warmly upon my thoughts, and indeed irresistibly, that now was my time to get me a servant, and perhaps a companion or assistant; and that I was called plainly by Providence to save this poor creature's life' (*ibid.,* 206).

In contrast, Tournier's Robinson attempts to kill Vendredi in order to save his own skin (literally), only the dog Tenn's sudden movement redirecting his shot to one of the pursuers. Robinson either feels no pressing need for company, or fails even to consider the Indian as a fellow-being. Earlier, he had longed for company of any form, friend or foe, to save him from madness. Now his wish is ironically granted.

It is striking that, in the first half of *Vendredi,* thoughts about the role and importance of *autrui* are couched almost exclusively in the form of abstract spatial metaphors. *Autrui* represents a different point of view, another perspective, a new centre of vision. In Chapter II, Robinson's failure with the *Évasion* is partly attributed to his oblivion to all but the immediate task at hand. Without *autrui,* another point of view, his vision is reduced to a single point:

> Il s'avisa ainsi qu'autrui est pour nous un puissant *facteur de distraction,* non seulement parce qu'il nous dérange sans cesse et nous arrache à notre pensée actuelle, mais aussi parce que la seule possibilité de sa survenue jette une vague lueur sur un univers d'objets situés en marge de notre attention, mais capable à tout moment d'en devenir le centre. (**36**)

In a log-book entry of Chapter III, Robinson expands on this notion, noting that other people 'constituent des points de vue possibles qui ajoutent au point de vue réel de l'observateur d'indispensables virtualités'. In his case, 'il n'y a qu'un point de vue, le mien, dépouillé de toute virtualité' (53). In the second half of the text, when these abstract statements are translated into a concrete situation, Robinson's ideas about *autrui* are forced to undergo a radical revision. Vendredi (and later, the men from the *Whitebird*) does indeed represent a new point of view, but rather than complement Robinson's perspective, he directly challenges it. The abstract metaphors failed to take into account one crucial factor: a new perspective does not necessarily reveal further aspects of the same 'reality'; it may disclose a quite different world.

Initially, Vendredi does reinforce Robinson's way of seeing, in much the same way as the island had done before him. If Robinson is to be Master, then Vendredi must be a servant. If he is a superior white Westerner, then Vendredi, in his eyes, must be the 'nègre', the half-caste who barely constitutes a human being. A humorous passage shortly after Vendredi's arrival reflects the manner in which the identity of the two men is interdependent. Making a philosophical point, the passage, with its hyperbolic accumulation of phrases, also serves as a parodic deflation of Robinson's colonial, ethnocentric views:

> Il est bien d'être soldat quand le maître est général, enfant de chœur quand il prie, maçon quand il construit, valet de ferme quand il se consacre à ses terres, berger quand il se préoccupe de ses troupeaux, rabatteur quand il chasse, pagayeur quand il vogue, porteur quand il voyage, guérisseur quand il souffre, et d'actionner pour lui l'éventail et le chasse-mouches. (149)

As long as Vendredi plays the game, accepting these roles, Robinson can sustain the various identities he has constructed for himself. The crunch comes when, for the first time, he is forced out of his egocentrism and, putting himself in Vendredi's place (the spatial metaphor again), he sees himself *through the Indian's eyes*. Earlier in the text as he looked into a mirror, he found that he could scarcely recognise himself (89). In *La Nausée*, Roquentin faces a similar situation, and attributes his experience to his isolation: 'Les autres qui vivent en société ont appris à se voir, dans les glaces, tels qu'ils apparaissent à leurs amis' (Sartre, 34). Now Robinson is no longer alone, but the mirror held up to his eyes by Vendredi does not show him what he wants to see:

> Alors je me mets à sa place, et je suis saisi de pitié devant cet enfant livré sans défense sur une île déserte à toutes les fantaisies d'un dément. Mais ma condition est pire encore, car je me vois dans mon unique compagnon sous les espèces d'un monstre, comme dans un miroir déformant. (155)

Rather than acting as a 'distraction' in the positive sense (the word stems from the Latin *dis-trahere,* to pull in different directions), Vendredi, by forcing Robinson to see differently, soon threatens to drive him to distraction. It is not only Robinson's perception of himself which is contested; he is also forced to reconsider his way of seeing the world about him. As well as openly deriding Robinson's westernised system, Vendredi represents a totally new approach. Native Indian skills can have their beneficial side. Vendredi disposes of Robinson's detritus by throwing it on a termite hill, and teaches his so-called master how to manipulate the bolas both to catch food and defend himself against potential enemies (**151-2**). For the most part, however, Robinson feels threatened by the radical otherness of his companion. He is both jealous of and slightly repulsed by Vendredi's closeness to Tenn. Discovering the Indian's hammock, raffia dolls, and bows and arrows, coming across the upturned trees which Vendredi has replanted, he is disturbed by this 'univers secret' (**163**).

In Chapter VIII, the contrast between the two men is accentuated further. Where the system-bound Robinson carefully labels each cactus plant with a Latin tag, Vendredi revels in the visual spectacle of the plants bedecked in European clothes and jewels (**158-9**). Free from Robinson's scrutiny (the gaze of the Other), Vendredi is no longer the servant but 'maître de lui, maître de l'île' (**157**). Hurling stones into the sea, he takes pleasure from the simple beauty of the natural world: 'La courbe du galet touchait en un seul point celle de sa paume noire, et formait avec elle une figure géométrique simple et pure' (**160**). Again, the text echoes *La Nausée:* Roquentin's first experience of nausea arises as he picks up a stone:

> Maintenant je me rappelle mieux ce que j'ai senti, l'autre jour, au bord de la mer, quand je tenais ce galet. C'était une espèce d'écœurement douceâtre. Que c'était donc desagréable! Et cela venait du galet, j'en suis sûr, cela passait du galet dans mes mains. Oui, c'est cela, c'est bien cela: une sorte de nausée dans mes mains. (Sartre, 24)

The textual echo once more points the way to a different way of seeing. Just as Robinson could appreciate the beauty of *l'autre île* without experiencing the fear of contingency or 'brute existence', so Vendredi can enjoy the existence of objects, free from functional or abstracting labels. Tournier again takes Sartre as his starting-point but turns what was seen as a terrifying and wholly negative perception of the world into a liberating experience.

Of course, it is not just Robinson who is shown a different way of seeing the world. Vendredi represents not only the Other, but a radically alien culture which serves to remind us of our own limited perspective. On a number of occasions, Vendredi's acts may disturb us as much as they do Robinson. When the Indian decides to make a shield from the carapace of a turtle, the incident is described in gruesome detail. As he hacks the creature's body from its shell the animal emits 'une sorte de toux rauque'. The turtle is left in a pitiful state: 'Une énorme cloque rouge, verte et violacée se balançait sur son dos comme une besace gonflée de sang et de fiel' (**170**). We may be equally repulsed by Vendredi's undertaking to feed a young vulture:

> Dès lors, l'Araucan laissa longuememt mûrir au soleil dans une nuée de mouches bleues des viscères de chevreau dont la puanteur exaspéra Robinson. Enfin des myriades de larves blanches grouillèrent dans la carne à demi liquifiée [...]. Puis il porta à sa bouche une pleine poignée d'asticots ainsi recueillis et mâcha patiemment, avec un air absent, l'immonde provende. Enfin, penché sur son protégé, il laissa couler dans son bec tendu comme une sébile d'aveugle une manière de lait épais et tiède que le vautour déglutit avec des frémissements de croupion. (**172-3**)

Passages such as these exemplify the manner in which *Vendredi* can elicit from us an ambivalent response. We do not wish to 'side' with Robinson-the-*Gouverneur*, the *vieil homme* who is too egocentric and too ethnocentric to see things differently. At the same time, we are perhaps uncomfortably aware that Vendredi's actions provoke our own disgust and condemnation. At such moments we share Robinson's point of view, and Tournier's text itself serves as a mirror held up to our limited point of view. We, like Robinson, may not like what we see.

The coexistence of two such different points of view, two ways of seeing the world, makes for a truly explosive situation. Something, or someone, must give, and after the blast it is Robinson who comes round to Vendredi's way of thinking (or seeing). From this point on his perceptions of both Vendredi and the island change. When Vendredi first arrives, he is regarded as practically subhuman. Robinson states: 'un sauvage n'est pas un être humain à part entière' (**147**). By Chapter X, Robinson's new point of view is clearly revealed as he says of Vendredi 'il est pour moi toute l'humanité rassemblée en un seul être' (**224**). The presence of *autrui* is now linked to the very condition of 'being human'. Earlier in the text Robinson rediscovers his capacity to smile—'la plus douce des facultés humaines'—only when the dog Tenn seems to grin at him in an almost human manner: *'Tenn souriait à son maître'* (**91**). Being human means being endowed with affective drives, and it is Vendredi, sole representative of all humankind, who enables Robinson to sustain his humanity: 'Que ferais-je de ma pitié et de ma haine, de mon admiration et de ma peur, si Vendredi ne m'inspirait pas en même temps pitié, haine, admiration et peur?' (**224**).

Robinson's relationship with Vendredi in the closing stages of the text is such that our earlier comments about the significance of *l'autre île* must be reconsidered. Robinson not only discovers 'another island', but

'un *autre Vendredi'* (**181**). Earlier in this chapter it was suggested that
the log-book entry discussing the redundancy of the categories of
subject and object (the 'état primaire de connaissance') referred to the
vision of *l'autre île*. And yet, in Chapter X, Robinson states: 'Cette autre
Speranza, j'y suis installé à demeure dans un "moment d'innocence" '
(**220**). Clearly there is an inconsistency here. If Robinson were
referring to a state in which the categories of self and other had broken
down, he would not be able to make the statement: as was suggested
above, such moments cannot be articulated. Equally, there is no
suggestion that the division between self and other as it applies to his
relationship with Vendredi has broken down: it is precisely because
Vendredi is distinct from Robinson, is *autrui,* that he can arouse pity,
anger or admiration in the castaway.

So what does Robinson mean when he says he is living in *l'autre île*
with 'un autre Vendredi'? The answer seems to be that whilst
maintaining the subject / object, self / other distinctions, he has learned to
see both Vendredi and the island free from reductive labels:

> Speranza n'est plus une terre inculte à faire fructifier, Vendredi n'est plus un
> sauvage qu'il est de mon devoir de morigéner. L'un et l'autre requièrent
> toute mon attention, une attention contemplative, une vigilance émerveillée,
> car il me semble — non, j'ai la certitude — que je les découvre à chaque
> instant pour la première fois et que rien ne ternit jamais leur magique
> nouveauté. (**220-21**)

This way of seeing, which as we have seen can be described in terms
of the heightened perception of a mystical experience, whilst not as
extreme as the position outlined in the log-book entry (**95-100**), does
represent a coming to terms with the existence of the Other (be it
another person or the world of objects) as existence, as autonomy, as
contingency. It was suggested above that this is the vision of the child.
The emphasis on 'newness', the purity of vision, the sheer fascination
which objects and other people exert over the child is also, according to
Baudelaire, characteristic of the inspired vision of the poet:

> L'enfant voit tout en *nouveauté;* il est toujours *ivre*. Rien ne ressemble plus
> à l'inspiration, que la joie avec laquelle l'enfant absorbe la forme et la
> couleur.

> C'est à cette curiosité profonde et joyeuse qu'il faut attribuer l'œil fixe et
> animalement extatique des enfants devant le *nouveau,* quel qu'il soit, visage
> ou paysage... (Baudelaire, 690)

It is precisely this attitude which we see exemplified in the log-book
entry of Chapter X. Robinson and Vendredi see with all the hungry
curiosity of the child, eager to absorb and touch, yet free from the as
yet unlearned, reductive labels which society imposes upon phenomena.

The parallels between the two texts are, in fact, striking. Vendredi subjects Robinson's body to a minute examination, scrutinising him 'avec une intensité extraordinaire', finally seizing his wrist and peering at 'une veine violette visible sous la peau nacrée' (**225**). This fascination is echoed in a reminiscence of Baudelaire:

> Un de mes amis me disait un jour qu'étant fort petit, il assistait à la toilette de son père, et qu'alors il contemplait, avec une stupeur mêlée de délices, les muscles des bras, les dégradations de couleurs de la peau nuancée de rose et de jaune, et le réseau bleuâtre des veines. (Baudelaire, 690-91)

Living in *l'autre île* means tearing away the veil of habit and convention. Robinson and Vendredi uncover, and discover, each other and the world about them as if for the first time every day.

The text, however, does not end here, and the equilibrium established is shattered by the arrival of the European ship, the *Whitebird*. Once again Vendredi stages a confrontation between two radically different points of view. The Western sailors bring with them their labelling, reductive vision. Just as Robinson saw himself through Vendredi's eyes before, so he now realises that from the ethnocentric perspective of the sailors Speranza is no more than an obscure island, whilst he and Vendredi are simply 'un naufragé nommé Robinson et son serviteur métis' (**238**). The egocentrism of the crew is such that they believe that their perspective represents the only possible, and the only correct, way of seeing: 'Aucun de ces hommes, murés dans leurs préoccupations particulières, ne songeait à l'interroger sur les péripéties qu'il avait traversée depuis son naufrage' (*ibid.*). At no point does it occur to them that a new perspective might contribute to their knowledge: 'Ses hôtes semblaient avoir admis une fois pour toutes qu'il avait tout à apprendre d'eux et rien à révéler sur lui-même et Vendredi' (**243**). To accept the point of view of the crew of the *Whitebird* would mean accepting their limited and limiting image of Robinson, his companion, and his world, and this is a step which he refuses to take.

A striking factor which arises from this incident is that Robinson is able to put himself in the place of the Westerners, to see through their eyes. This is something which Vendredi cannot do. Unlike Robinson, the Indian does not have sufficient knowledge of Western culture to understand that his departure from Speranza will end in slavery. We, like Robinson, are aware of the fate which awaits Vendredi. Earlier in the text the mate of the *Whitebird* had told Robinson about the growing slave trade, so that when Jaan informs him that Vendredi 'est entré chez le second qui paraissait l'attendre' (**252**) we, like him, put two and two together. At this point in our reading, we are therefore closer to Robinson, whose point of view we share. Vendredi's failure to see once again emphasises his radical Otherness.

This fact emphasises the tensions inherent to the text. In a sense, Tournier is faced with something of a dilemma. Inasmuch as he is writing a novel which decries ethnocentrism and invites us to see differently, he must both allow us to see something of ourselves in Robinson and at the same time reveal the inadequacies of his protagonist. We must be both complicit with and distanced from Robinson. Equally, he must show us a different perspective represented by Vendredi. But which perspective, whose point of view finally prevails? Though the title of the text suggests that its true protagonist is Vendredi, is it not with Robinson that our sympathies often lie? Paradoxically, the very otherness of Vendredi may be such that the reader remains alienated from him. Whilst complicity with Robinson is achieved by means of the first-person log-book, Vendredi, as suggested above in Chapter Two, remains a closed book, presented primarily via his actions and, occasionally, his words. Furthermore, even though Robinson is forced to shed much of his Western mind-set, and though we may be led to assume that he will, in some form or other, teach Jaan to appreciate his new lifestyle, the fact remains that by the close of the text it is two white, Western characters who remain on the island.

In response to a reader asking him why he had not dedicated *Vendredi* to Defoe, Tournier confided that he had, in fact, had another dedication in mind, though he had refrained from using it:

> Oui, j'aurais voulu dédier ce livre à la masse énorme et silencieuse des travailleurs immigrés de France, tous ces Vendredi dépêchés vers nous par le tiers monde [...]. Notre société de consommation est assise sur eux, elle a posé ses fesses grasses et blanches sur ce peuple basané réduit au plus absolu silence. Tous ces éboueurs, ces fraiseurs, ces terrassiers, ces manoeuvres, ces trimardeurs, il va de soi qu'ils n'ont rien à dire, rien à nous apprendre, tout à gagner au contraire à notre école et d'abord à apprendre à parler une langue civilisée, celle de Descartes, de Corneille et de Pasteur, à acquérir des manières policées, et surtout à se faire oublier des stupides et bornés Robinson que nous sommes tous. (*VP*, 236-7)

Perhaps the true lesson to be learned from *Vendredi* is not that we should radically change our point of view, but that we should learn to put ourselves in the place of *autrui,* to appreciate that another perspective is possible, to be receptive, as far as that is possible, to another person's, or another culture's way of seeing. The difficulty with this is that to do so may not always be possible. In the artificial setting of a desert island, Robinson is willing, and able, to learn from Vendredi. This, as Tournier suggests, is the obvious course of action:

> Car pour vivre sur une île du Pacifique ne vaut-il pas mieux se mettre à l'école d'un indigène rompu à toutes les techniques adaptées à ce milieu particulier que de s'acharner à plaquer sur elle un mode de vie purement anglais? (*VP*, 227-8)

But the reverse situation highlights the limitations of the argument. When Vendredi goes off to the West it seems unlikely that he will learn from the Westerners, or they from him. Learning from *autrui* may be possible, and it is certainly desirable, but the will and capability must be there on both sides.

# Chapter Six

# Structuring the Text

> Pour que mes romans puissent remplir la fonction que je leur ai assignée—celle
> d'un marteau-piqueur servant à défoncer le réel pour découvrir ce qui
> se cache en dessous, il faut qu'ils constituent un ensemble absolument
> cohérent, une 'Gestalt' dont les parties se répondent les unes aux autres.

Thus Tournier in an interview, and that he should take *Vendredi ou les limbes du Pacifique* as the title of his Robinson Crusoe story indicates a shift of emphasis which is mirrored at this important structural level, specifically, in the proportion of text devoted to Vendredi. While two thirds of Defoe's text focuses on Crusoe's life prior to Friday's arrival, with less than one tenth—or 25 of some 270 pages—covering the period which the two men spend alone together, *Vendredi* falls into two sections of approximately equal length, six chapters depicting Robinson alone on Speranza and six describing his life after he is joined by Vendredi, four of these preceding the account of the arrival of the *Whitebird*. Although we never learn exactly how long Robinson and Vendredi are together, the narrative comment that 'des années durant, il avait été à la fois le maître et le père de Vendredi' (**191**) suggests a fairly extensive period of time. Defoe's Crusoe, in sharp contrast, spends less than three of his twenty-eight years on the island in the company of Friday. These structural differences are a clear reflection of the contrasting aims of the two novels. In *Vendredi*, Tournier sets up one system in the first half of the text and then subverts it; the Araucanian Indian's way of life and values constitute a challenge and an alternative to Robinson's Western European approach. Vendredi's arrival, at a crisis-point, establishes a pattern of 'before' and 'after':

> Les deux volets de Robinson sur son île, *Avant-Vendredi, Avec-Vendredi*,
> s'articulent parfaitement l'un sur l'autre, le drame de la solitude s'exhalant
> dans un appel à un compagnon, puis se trouvant soudain étouffé, suffoqué
> par la survenue d'un compagnon en effet, mais inattendu, surprenant, une
> déception affreuse—un nègre!—contenant pourtant toutes les promesses
> d'une relance prodigieuse de l'aventure et de l'invention. (*VP*, 232)

In *Robinson Crusoe* there is no such crisis and no real 'relance prodigieuse'. If there is no need to devote half of the text to Crusoe's life with Friday it is because the function of the Indian is not to introduce a viable alternative lifestyle, but to affirm the order established in the section of the text devoted to the hero's solitary struggles. Crusoe does not need time—in terms of textual space—to change, because it is he who is going to transform Friday. Indeed, the sheer brevity of the period required to convert Friday to his way of life underlines the apparent supremacy and worth of the ideology which Crusoe represents. As soon as Friday conforms, the tale threatens to lose impetus, and Defoe picks up the pace by introducing new characters and events in the form first of native 'savages' and their two prisoners, a Spaniard and (rather extraordinarily) Friday's father, then of an English ship full of mutineering sailors. The final section of the text recounts Crusoe's return journey to England.

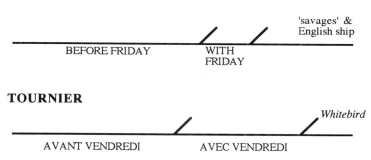

**DEFOE**

'savages' &
English ship

BEFORE FRIDAY      WITH FRIDAY

**TOURNIER**

*Whitebird*

AVANT VENDREDI      AVEC VENDREDI

Looking at *Vendredi* as a binary structure means emphasising one particular aspect of the text, namely the change in direction precipitated by Vendredi's arrival. Certainly two distinct sections of text can be distinguished, but in fact, the majority of significant changes take place after the explosion of gunpowder triggered off by Vendredi's illicit pipe-smoking. Although the Indian's arrival is situated midway through the text, if we are looking for a two-fold structure, the principal point of articulation is thus perhaps best situated between Chapters VIII and IX. It is from this point on that Robinson, previously master, sheds his coloniser's mentality, and follows Vendredi's lead. Speranza is no longer regarded as an area of land to be cultivated and regulated, nor as a sexual partner or Other who can confirm Robinson in his dominant malehood. The prevailing element earth gives way to air and finally fire. Robinson discards the Bible and chooses to listen to the 'inner voice' of the Holy Ghost; he overcomes his puritanical distaste for his own body. Changes extend to the narrative patterning of the text: prior to the explosion, Robinson's split personality is reflected in the alternation of the first-person log-book and the third-person narrative within individual chapters; from Chapter IX to the end of the text each chapter is narrated wholly in one or the other mode.

A model of this sort is of course by its very nature a simplification, and though it is by no means invalid, it is highly reductive. If this chapter is entitled 'structuring the text' (as opposed, say, to 'textual structures') it is in order to acknowledge the fact that the identification of structures is based on a process of selection: structures only 'work'—are convincing—to the extent that we choose to focus on certain textual elements to the exclusion of others. Tournier can only choose to name the second *volet* in his binary model *Avec-Vendredi,* for instance, by disregarding the fact that Vendredi is (at least physically) absent from the final chapter of the text. (The narrator's claim that Robinson 'ne devait plus lâcher cette main brune qui avait saisi la sienne' (**190**) might be taken to suggest that Vendredi lives on on the island, if only to the extent that his way of life has been assimilated by Robinson himself.) Furthermore, the *relance* which comprises the second half of *Vendredi* is interrupted in Chapter XI by the arrival of the ship. The sections could be better named *avant autrui / avec autrui.*

If the second section of *Vendredi* can be subdivided in order to acknowledge events which produce significant changes (the departure of Vendredi, for instance), the same process can be extended to the first six chapters. Tournier proposes a ternary model, breaking the text down into three sections: *la souille* (Chapters I and II); *l'île administrée* (Chapters III to VIII); *l'extase solaire* (Chapters IX to XII). Always eager to suggest that his works are open to different levels of interpretation, Tournier points out that the three stages of Robinson's development correspond to three paths open to each of us in our daily life: 'les plaisirs purement passifs et dégradants—l'alcool, la drogue'; 'le travail et l'ambition sociale'; 'la pure contemplation artistique ou religieuse'. To this he adds a metaphysical stratum, noting that the ternary division also corresponds to the three types of knowledge discussed in Spinoza's *Ethics:*

> La connaissance du premier genre passe par les sens et les sentiments, et se caractérise par sa subjectivité, sa fortuité et son immédiateté. A la connaissance du deuxième genre correspondent les sciences et les techniques. C'est une connaissance rationnelle mais superficielle, médiate et largement utilitaire. Seule la connaissance du troisième genre livre l'absolu dans une intuition de son essence. (*VP,* 235)

Whilst these authorial comments may provide new insights into the text, perhaps of greater interest is Tournier's claim that the ternary structure lends *Vendredi* 'une allure dialectique': in other words, the final section can be seen as a synthesis of the previous two, which themselves represent opposing or contradictory elements. Though Tournier does not elaborate on this observation, a dialectical movement can be detected in Robinson's attitude to order and time.

In the course of the first section (*la souille*), Robinson makes no attempt to transform his surroundings. The natural world prevails, and this world, as Robinson later comments, is in his eyes the epitome of *disorder:* 'Ma victoire, c'est l'ordre moral que je dois imposer à Speranza contre son ordre naturel qui n'est que l'autre nom du désordre absolu' (**50**). Closely linked to Robinson's perception of order / disorder is his attitude to time. During the period of the *souille* he fails to keep track of the passing days and consequently has the disorienting and depressing impression that he is living in a continuous present:

> Il convient d'ajouter qu'ayant négligé de tenir un calendrier depuis le naufrage, il n'avait qu'une idée vague du temps qui s'écoulait. Les jours se superposaient, tous pareils, dans sa mémoire, et il avait le sentiment de recommencer chaque matin la journée de la veille. (**27**)

This state of affairs is reversed in the second section as the natural world is subjected to a rigorous ordering process; all natural phenomena must be classified and labelled, strict rules must be established as Robinson seeks to impose his system and combat the threatening otherness of the island. A calendar is established and a water-clock constructed. Time too is now kept in check, every minute of every day accounted for: 'Désormais, que je veille ou que je dorme, que j'écrive ou que je fasse la cuisine, mon temps est sous-tendu par un tic-tac machinal, objectif, irréfutable, exact, contrôlable' (**67**).

If the first section can be labelled 'disorder' and the second 'order', the third provides the synthesis of these two positions. Before Vendredi's arrival, Robinson cannot see beyond the alternatives of the despair of the *souille* and his manic ordering and controlling, both of which he comes to perceive as unsatisfactory. Vendredi holds the key to a new order, a new way of seeing, and a different way of living, or experiencing, time. Though his days are totally unplanned, and though—or rather because—he lives 'enfermé dans l'instant présent' (**190**), the Indian's way of life represents a liberation far removed from either the order or the disorder previously experienced by Robinson:

> La liberté de Vendredi [...] n'était pas que la négation de l'ordre effacé de la surface de l'île par l'explosion. Robinson savait trop bien, par le souvenir de ses premiers temps à Speranza, ce qu'était une vie désemparée, errant à la dérive et soumise à toutes les impulsions du caprice et à toutes les retombées du découragement, pour ne pas pressentir une unité cachée, un principe implicite dans la conduite de son compagnon. (*ibid.*)

By the close of the text, Robinson, like his pupil-turned-teacher, lives in and for the present. When he comes to state 'il me semble revivre sans cesse la même journée' (**219**), he means it in a wholly positive sense.

| LA SOUILLE | | | | *L'ILE ADMINISTRÉE* | | | | | L'EXTASE SOLAIRE | | |
|---|---|---|---|---|---|---|---|---|---|---|---|
| 1 | 2 | 3 | 4 | 5 | 6 | 7 | 8 | 9 | 10 | 11 | 12 |

| l'*Évasion* | *Robinson-Gouverneur-administrateur-général* | Vendredi meneur de jeu |
|---|---|---|
| l'alcool, la drogue | *le travail et l'ambition sociale* | la pure contemplation artistique ou religieuse |
| DÉSORDRE | *ORDRE* | NOUVEL ORDRE |
| recommencer chaque matin la journée de la veille | *ainsi le niveau du liquide donnait l'heure à tout moment* | revivre sans cesse la même journée |

Moving from a binary to a ternary model in effect means narrowing the focus, breaking the text down into ever smaller sections in order to take into account more precisely defined stages of Robinson's development. This process can be extended to a six-fold structure dividing *Vendredi* into pairs of chapters, each pairing conforming to a set pattern: a theme or stage of development is introduced in the first chapter of the pairing, then amplified or intensified in the second. In Chapter I, the despondent Robinson plans the construction of his escape-vessel; in Chapter II, the ship is built, cannot be launched, and Robinson's despair deepens. Chapter III sees the initiation of his administrative and agricultural projects which are then extended to include the fortifications, Charter and Penal Code of Chapter IV, etc.

| 1 | 2 | 3 | 4 | 5 | 6 |
|---|---|---|---|---|---|
| l'île de la Désolation | | Speranza | | l'île-femme | |
| chasse cueillette | échec de l'*Évasion* la souille | Robinson agriculteur administrateur | Charte Code pénal fortifications | la grotte l'île-mère | la combe l'île-épouse |

| 7 | 8 | 9 | 10 | 11 | 12 |
|---|---|---|---|---|---|
| nouveau point de vue conflit | | la vie sauvage | | perte et regain | |
| maître / esclave | l'univers secret | un corps accepté jeux aériens | célébration log-book | *Whitebird* | Jaan |

The geometric, rather mechanistic structural models proposed so far serve their purpose, revealing the broad movements of the text, the 'wide-angle' view (to return to the photographic metaphor). As we proceed from one model to another, we see with increasing clarity that the changes which Robinson undergoes are not abrupt; the gradual nature of his transformation from *vieil homme* to *homme nouveau* is represented with greater accuracy. As an earlier chapter of this study has indicated, elements of change—or the potential for change—are apparent as early as Chapter II, when Robinson first experiences a sense of communion with the natural elements; the last vestiges of the *vieil homme* —'ce qui demeure en moi du dévot puritain que je fus' (**228**)—are discernible as late as Chapter X. The organic imagery which is used on a number of occasions to describe Robinson's evolution—the butterfly or 'larve' emerging from the chrysalis (**94**; **226**); the embryonic 'cosmos en gestation' (**117**)—points to the slow, but inevitable nature of the metamorphic process, which can be represented schematically by means of converging and diverging lines:

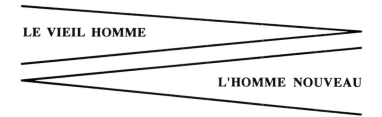

**LE VIEIL HOMME**

**L'HOMME NOUVEAU**

The models proposed so far all have one thing in common: they take Chapter I as the starting-point of the text and establish the final chapter as a definitive end-point. *Vendredi,* however, does not begin with Chapter I, but with the italicised prologue. The remainder of this chapter will focus on two structural models which take this prologue into account, the first of these centring on Captain Van Deyssel's prophetic reading of Robinson's cards.

The tarot pack, generally thought to have originated in fourteenth-century Europe—the word 'tarot' stems from the Italian 'tarocco', a card game played with the tarot deck—consists of 78 cards, 56 Minor Arcana divided into four suits of 14 cards (numbered 1 to 10 with a King, Queen, Cavalier and Page), and 22 Major Arcana. Readings may be carried out using either the full spread of cards or, as is the case in *Vendredi,* the Major Arcana alone. Each of these cards, numbered I to

XXI with an additional un-numbered card representing the Fool (*Le Mat*), has a title and a symbolic picture upon which the interpreter bases his or her reading. Because Van Deyssel provides his own interpretive gloss, the reader of *Vendredi* need not be familiar with the symbolic significance of the cards turned up by Robinson, and the following discussion remains strictly within the confines of the information supplied in the prologue. (For a fuller discussion of the tarot card reading, see Sbiroli.) The cards are not always given their traditional tarot titles by the Captain, so for those readers who might wish to pursue the matter further, these have been supplied where necessary.

The most important feature—or function—of the tarot reading is that it prompts us, as readers, actively to seek structures, to establish links between Van Deyssel's cryptic commentary and the events which take place in the main body of the text. There are eleven cards, so we naturally assume that *Vendredi* can be divided into eleven phases or sections. This process, however, is by no means straightforward, as the following discussion will demonstrate.

When we first read the prologue we probably realise at once that the tarot reading provides us with an encoded representation or prefiguration of the events which unfold in the following chapters. However, we, like Robinson, are not given 'une prévision lucide de l'avenir' (**13**) in the sense of 'knowing what will happen'; at most we may form a shadowy impression of a pattern of success and failure. As we begin to read the main text, a two-way process is set in motion. Gradually the captain's cryptic comments start to make sense and the significance of the cards is decoded: in other words, the main text allows us retrospectively to interpret the contents of the prologue. At the same time, if we refer back to the prologue, Van Deyssel's comments can be fed into the main text, granting us greater understanding of the significance of various events. Some connections between the prologue and Robinson's life on Speranza are more straightforward than others, and we can begin by looking at the four cards whose significance can most easily be grasped.

When Robinson retreats into the 'womb' of Speranza in Chapter V, we retrospectively make the connection with the third tarot card, *L'Hermite* (Arcana IX). At the same time, Van Deyssel's comments provide information which can be channelled back into our reading: Robinson's act represents a search for his roots (he enters the cavern 'pour y retrouver sa source originelle'); the experience is akin to a rebirth, a fundamental transformation—'il est devenu un autre homme' (**8**). The ninth card figures two children holding hands in front of a wall representing the 'Cité solaire' (*Le Soleil,* Arcana XIX). We learn that this card is associated with a particular conception of time—the 'Cité solaire' is 'suspendu entre le temps et l'éternité'—and sexuality—

the 'sexualité solaire'. This information (these clues) allow us to relate the card to Robinson's log-book entry in Chapter X in which he discusses his new-found attitudes to time and gender differentiation at some length. Van Deyssel adds to the information supplied by Robinson: the 'extase solaire' is associated with the innocence of children; it represents 'le zénith de la perfection humaine' (12). The tenth card, *La Mort* (Arcana XIII), is clearly linked to the arrival of the *Whitebird* in Chapter XI; the cabin-boy Jaan is represented by the last card, the 'enfant d'or, issu des entrailles de la terre' (*Le Jugement*, Arcana XX).

The rest of the cards are more intriguing; we may find it difficult to establish a one-to-one link between each one and a particular event or even section of text. The 'démiurge' or *Bateleur* (Arcana I) who seeks to impose order 'avec des moyens de fortune' seems to point to the planning and building of the *Évasion* in Chapters I and II, to a stage in Robinson's development when he is confident that he will succeed (we learn that the figure is as yet unaware that 'son oeuvre est illusion, son ordre est illusoire'). At the same time, the significance of the card extends beyond a specific incident: the *bateleur* or *démiurge* represents a facet of Robinson's character—his desire to organise— which is very much in evidence throughout the whole of the first half of the text. The crowned figure in the chariot (*Le Chariot*, Arcana VII) who wins an apparent victory over nature relates to the administrative endeavours of Chapters III and IV. This time it is Van Deyssel's acerbic criticism of Robinson's character which provide us with useful information: if Robinson fails it is because he is too pure, too austere, and above all, too sure of himself.

*L'Hermite,* as we have seen, can be connected to Robinson's explorations of the *grotte;* beyond this, the card represents that stage of Robinson's development during which he seeks to establish his relationship with the element earth: in other words, the whole of Chapters V and VI, encompassing the *voie végétale* and the *combe rose*. The fourth card can be identified by Van Deyssel's description as *L'Étoile* (Arcana XVII): 'Voilà qui va faire sortir l'Hermite de son trou! Vénus en personne émerge des eaux et fait ses premiers pas sur vos plate-bandes' (9). The expression 'marcher sur les plate-bandes' signifies an intrusion into someone else's domain, and seems to point to the difficult transitionary period of Chapters VII and VIII. Later in the text Robinson himself comments on the role Vendredi has played in turning him away from the earth (the period of the *île épouse*) to the air and fire (sun), referring to 'l'homme de la terre arraché de son trou par le génie éolien' (226). In card five, Venus (Vendredi), now transformed into a winged angel shooting arrows towards the sky (*L'Amoureux,* Arcana VI), reminds us of Vendredi's archery in Chapter IX, but may also refer more generally to Robinson's gradual movement towards the *extase solaire.* The Venus figure returns in the eighth card (*Le Diable,* Arcana XV) in the guise of 'frère jumeau', allowing us to link the card to the period which follows the explosion and precedes the arrival of the *Whitebird.*

The sixth and seventh cards prove to be rather more problematic. From Van Deyssel's interjection—'Malheur!'—we assume that the card named 'Chaos' (*Le Monde,* Arcana XXI), heralds a downturn in Robinson's fortunes. The captain's enigmatic words become ever more obscure (and rather reminiscent of the coded messages broadcast on the radio during the Second World War!): 'La bête de la Terre est en lutte avec un monstre de flammes' (**9**). To what does this refer? Because the cards so far have unfolded chronologically in relation to the events of the main text, we may be reluctant to link this to the explosion which comes at the end of Chapter VIII (since the previous card seemed to relate to Chapter IX). In any case, the card relates to a point in time when Robinson is still 'pris entre des forces opposées'; in other words, to the period which precedes the explosion. A similar ambiguity surrounds the seventh card, *Le Pendu* (Arcana XII). Van Deyssel's slightly mocking observation—'vous voilà donc la tête en bas, mon pauvre Crusoé'—again seems to suggest a period of struggle and confusion. Is the inversion a reference to Vendredi's uprooting of trees in Chapter VIII? Or to the handstands turned by Robinson in Chapter IX? There are no clear-cut answers to these question and it would be wrong to suggest that there are. We, like the *Bateleur,* seek to impose order; like Robinson himself we are forced to reflect upon our desire to find meaning, to structure, and we may be forced to acknowledge that our attempts may not be successful. One cannot help feeling that Tournier, like Van Deyssel, would take an amused pleasure in our efforts.

Whether we choose to consider *Vendredi* in terms of a binary or ternary construction, greater or smaller subdivisions of text, the common feature shared by these models is their essentially linear conception of the novel. When Vendredi arrives, Robinson is launched into a new world of discovery which replaces his past way of life. The third section of the text, the *extase solaire,* represents a synthesis of the preceding two sections; each pairing of chapters points to a step in Robinson's journey to the 'Cité solaire'. To some extent the tarot reading in the prologue challenges that linear conception, if only because it reveals to us our desire to establish a chronological connection between the cards and the main text; a desire which is probably thwarted. A second structural model which takes the presence of the prologue into account provides a much more direct challenge to the linear models considered so far.

In his work *The Myth of the Eternal Return,* Mircea Eliade examines

two different conceptions of time held respectively by modern man and
by members of archaic or traditional societies: primitive man (the term
is used with no derogatory connotations). Summing up and simplifying
what is in fact a complex discussion of the evolution of the modern
viewpoint, we can say that for modern man, strongly influenced by the
Judaeo-Christian tradition, time is essentially linear and irreversible;
man is caught up in the ongoing, one-way process of history. It is
precisely this conception of time which we can see reflected in the
structure of *Robinson Crusoe*.

As we read Defoe's text we are constantly aware of process, of the
passing of time. The very first words—'I was born in the year
1632'—anchor the story in a temporal continuum. From this point on
Crusoe repeatedly reminds us of the passing years: it is in 1651 that he
sets out on a first sea voyage from Hull to London; the shipwreck
strands him on the island in 1659; as the story unfolds Crusoe tells us
that one, then two, four, eleven, fifteen, eighteen, twenty-three years
have gone by. The European ship arrives in the twenty-seventh year of
his twenty-eight-year stay; Crusoe leaves the island in 1686, reaching
England in 1687. With the closing words of the text Crusoe projects us
forwards into the future, hinting at further adventures to come: 'all
these things, with some very surprising incidents in some new
adventures of my own, for ten years more, I may perhaps give a farther
account of hereafter' (*RC*, 299). From start to finish the linear, ongoing
nature of time, of Crusoe's unfolding story, is brought to our attention.

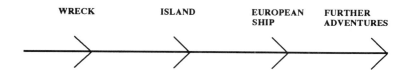

**LINEAR, HISTORICAL TIME**

Primitive man, unlike his modern counterpart, has what Eliade
refers to as an anti-historical conception of time. For the man of archaic
or traditional societies, history can be abolished, duration suspended, in
two principal ways. In the mythical past (*in illo tempore*—in those days)
gods, heroes and ancestors carried out certain acts. When primitive man
takes part in activities which have a mythical prototype—acts which
may be formal and ceremonious such as sacrifices, or more mundane,
for example play, hunting, eating, building—these take place, in his
eyes, at the primordial mythical moment: time, duration, history are

consequently suspended; the mythical instant and the present moment are conflated. The repetition of paradigmatic or archetypal acts takes place in what Eliade refers to as 'sacred' time, the only reality: acts and gestures acquire reality, become meaningful, only to the extent that they repeat a primordial act. The rest of primitive man's life (when he is not engaged in the repetition of mythical acts) takes place in 'profane' time, which is meaningless and unreal. Time can also be suspended, duration and history abolished, by means of periodic regeneration. Both formal ceremonies and simple acts which signify a beginning—forming a pot, for example, or lighting a fire—may effectively bring one cycle to a close and inaugurate another; time starts over again.

If *Robinson Crusoe* reflects a modern conception of time, *Vendredi* points to a primitive, anti-historical stance. When Robinson starts out, when the modern, Western *vieil homme* of the *île administrée* prevails, he has a typically linear conception of time:

> Jadis chaque journée, chaque heure, chaque minute était inclinée en quelque sorte vers la journée, l'heure ou la minute suivante, et toutes ensemble étaient aspirées par le dessein du moment dont l'inexistence provisoire créait comme un vacuum. Ainsi le temps passait vite et utilement, d'autant plus vite qu'il était plus utilement employé, et il laissait derrière lui un amas de monuments et de détritus qui s'appelait mon histoire. [...] ma courte vie était pour moi un segment rectiligne dont les deux bouts pointaient absurdement vers l'infini... (**218**)

As he sheds his Western mentality and comes under the influence of Vendredi in the period of the *extase solaire,* this linear viewpoint changes: in Chapter X, Robinson points out that in the past cyclical time remained 'le secret des dieux'; now, however, time has become an accelerated cycle—'le cycle s'est rétréci au point qu'il se confond avec l'instant' (**219**)—in such a way that he feels that he is living in a perpetual present. Time is suspended for him just as it is for primitive man:

> The life of archaic man [...] although it takes place in time, does not bear the burden of time, does not record time's irreversibility; in other words, completely ignores what is especially characteristic and decisive on a consciousness of time. Like the mystic, like the religious man in general, the primitive lives in a continual present. (Eliade, 1989: 86)

Robinson's perception of timelessness is directly linked to the rising sun: 'Chaque matin était pour lui comme un premier commencement' (**246**). As Eliade has observed, the sunrise, marking the beginning of a new day, is often associated with a rebirth, a new beginning:

> The sun, plunging every evening into the darkness of death and into the primordial waters, symbol of the uncreated and the virtual, resembles both

> the embryo in the womb and the neophyte hidden in the initiatory hut. When the sun rises in the morning, the world is reborn, just as the initiate emerges from his hut. (Eliade, 1975: 59)

The fact that Robinson should climb up a mountain to greet the new day is itself significant. In his discussion of the primitive mind-set Eliade points to the importance of 'cosmic centres', sacred places where the cosmogony, the Creation of the world, was deemed to have taken place. These centres or *axes mundi*, representing the meeting of heaven and earth, both the highest point and the navel of the world, often take the form of mountains. It has already been suggested that the description of Robinson bathed in sunlight on the summit of the *chaos* echoes the Transfiguration of Christ on Mount Tabor. Eliade (1989: 13) suggests that Tabor could mean 'tabbur', or 'navel', and it is surely no coincidence that the rocky outcrop or *chaos*, the highest point on Speranza, is formed from the *grotte*, or womb of Speranza ('A la place de la grotte—dont l'entrée avait disparu—s'élevait un chaos de blocs gigantesques'— **186**). When Robinson stands atop the mountainous *chaos*, he starts his life anew: attaining the centre, Eliade states, 'is equivalent to a consecration, an initiation; yesterday's profane and illusory existence gives way to a new existence, to a life that is real, enduring, and effective' (Eliade, 1989: 18).

If we consider *Vendredi* from the perspective of the opposition between archaic and modern conceptions of time, and include the prologue in our structural considerations, Tournier's novel, like the serpent swallowing its own tail in Van Deyssel's prophecy, can be seen to assume a circular form. Unlike *Robinson Crusoe*, dates are mentioned only twice in *Vendredi*, and the location of these temporal markers is significant. It is in the prologue that we learn that Robinson's ill-fated voyage begins on 29 September 1759 (**10**). Once we enter the main body of the text, we, like Robinson, lose track of the passing years: neither dates nor precise references to the amount of time which Robinson has spend on the island are provided until Chapter XI. Only at this point, when the first mate of the *Whitebird* informs Robinson that it is 29 December 1787, do we discover, perhaps with as much astonishment as Robinson, that twenty-eight years have elapsed. The European ship brings with it an abrupt influx of time; suddenly both we and Robinson are aware of the passing of the years, of process and duration. Linear time returns, and with it the horrors of history: Captain Hunter tells Robinson tales of greed, slavery and war (**238**).

Usually, in desert-island tales, the arrival of a second ship heralds the close of the text. This is a time for rescue and the vindication of Western (mainland) values: the relieved castaway departs from the island and returns home, often leaving a replica of Western society behind him. In the case of *Vendredi*, however, this is not the end of the story (though it may be the end of history). Tournier inverts, and thus subverts, the traditional rescue motif: Robinson stays on Speranza. The structure of *Vendredi* signals a rejection not only of Western values, but of a linear conception of time, which is first excluded from the text by being annexed in the prologue, then reintroduced only to be structurally subsumed as the text continues to a twelfth chapter. At the same time, the text makes a stand against the tradition of the desert-island story: the motif of the shipwreck, the traditional beginning of the island scenario, is relegated to the prologue, excluded from the main part of the text; the rescue ship is ousted from its usual function of bringing the tale of island life to a close. These structural features are represented below:

**PROLOGUE**

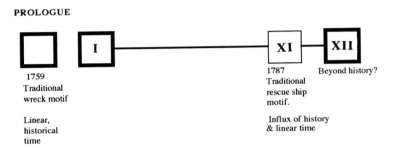

1759
Traditional
wreck motif

Linear,
historical
time

1787
Traditional
rescue ship
motif.

Beyond history?

Influx of history
& linear time

This model requires further elaboration: the structure of *Vendredi* does more than point to a rejection of linear time, it indicates an alternative, circular conception. A number of elements point to this circular model. A new beginning is strongly signalled by repetition: in the first chapter, Robinson climbs to the highest point of the island and surveys his surroundings (18); by Chapter XII he has come full circle, ascending the *chaos* to see the very same view. The arrival of the cabin-boy Jaan also heralds a new beginning: this time it is Robinson who will be leader and teacher, as a new life begins for the two of them. Finally, the very fact that there are twelve chapters is significant: when Robinson muses upon the secrets of timelessness, he states:

> Pourtant certains indices nous enseignent qu'il y a des clefs pour l'éternité: l'almanach, par exemple, dont les saisons sont un éternel retour à l'échelle humaine, et même la modeste ronde des heures. (**218-19**)

Twelve months in each year, twelve hours marking out the cycle of day and night and twelve chapters signalling a new beginning to Robinson's story:

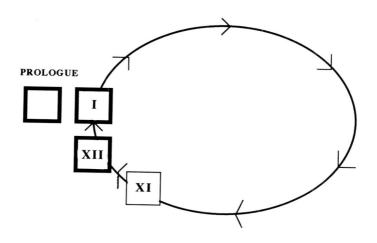

PROLOGUE

Unlike the linear structural models, the circular schema establishes Chapter XII not as an ending, but as a stage in a cyclical trajectory. However, whereas a circle usually suggests endless repetition, the ending of *Vendredi* leaves us speculating, projecting into a fictitious future as we consider what form Robinson's new life with Jaan might take. Van Deyssel's indication that the 'Cité solaire' is 'infiniment difficile à conquérir, plus difficile encore à garder' (**12**) leaves us wondering. His reading is, after all, interrupted after eleven cards have been turned up: would a twelfth card have signalled further change? Is another fall from grace on the cards? One further detail hints at the possibility of change. When Robinson names Vendredi after a day of the week he comments on his choice: 'Ce n'est ni un nom de personne, ni un nom commun, c'est, à mi-chemin entre les deux, celui d'une entité abstraite, fortement marquée par son caractère *temporel, fortuit et comme épisodique*' (**148**; my emphasis). Does Robinson's selection of the name 'Jeudi' for Jaan not also point to the possibility of change? 'Fortuit: ce qui arrive ou semble arriver par hasard, d'une manière imprévue', says the dictionary: we are left wondering if another unexpected event is not just over the horizon. The ambiguities surrounding the end of *Vendredi* allow us to propose one final structural model, a circle which is open-ended: in other words, a spiral.

# Conclusion

The opening pages of this study cited Tournier's observation that a text is brought to life by the reading act. The closed book, the printed text set down by the author, is only one half of the 'mélange inextricable' which constitutes the literary work. In the Introduction it was also stated that Tournier weaves strands from different disciplines into his novel. This claim, of course, raises a moot point: are these various strands of philosophy, ethnology, unorthodox spirituality, and so forth, present in the text, or are they rather brought to it by the reader, who interprets the printed words according to his or her own intellectual repertoire (or 'infrastructure', to use Tournier's term)? Even to begin to answer this question would, I fear, be to engage with a theoretical debate whose many ramifications would lead me far beyond the scope of this study. Taking what is perhaps the coward's way out, therefore, I would simply say that whatever school of thought we may wish to adhere to, *Vendredi ou les limbes du Pacifique* is a text which is particularly open to different interpretations.

Now that we have come to the end of this study it will have become apparent that the various strands of thought do not lie, as it were, side by side, but criss-cross and overlap. Changing the metaphor slightly, we might say that a number of interpretive grids can be laid over the text, and that these grids form nodal points where different interpretations converge. Thus the *extase solaire* is associated with the heightened state of awareness of the mystic, the inspired vision of the poet, the purity of perception of the child. It marks the final stage in the protagonist's journey through the four natural elements, but also harks back to his Quaker roots, representing the unorthodox spirituality of the Third Age of the Holy Ghost. To this can be added or superimposed interpretive grids from philosophical and ethnological or anthropological disciplines. Robinson's acceptance of the inherent 'otherness' of the natural world, his breaking away from reductive labelling and categorising, echoes but alters Sartrean ideas: an awareness of 'brute existence' becomes a liberating rather than a threatening experience. The suggestion that time has been suspended on the island of the *extase solaire* period points to a primitive or archaic conception of time, to periodic regeneration ceremonies and initiatory rebirth.

Isolated incident and events are open to the same plurality of interpretation. Vendredi's pursuit and victory over the he-goat Andoar represents the primitive man's radically different attitude to the animal kingdom, and is thematically opposed to Robinson's westernised and 'civilised' farming and domestication projects. At the same time, the reader who is familiar with the Selkirk accounts and *Robinson Crusoe* can see how Tournier has developed what was originally a factual incident, grafting onto it the sense of threat and evil present in Defoe's text, then bringing to his own version a symbolic aspect. Andoar represents the earth-bound Robinson who, under Vendredi's influence, will progress from the element earth to air and fire, as Andoar will be transformed into a kite and an aeolian harp. More than this, the Andoar story ties in with biblical motifs. Described in terms of an Old Testament figure ('il vit se pencher sur lui un masque de patriarche sémite'— **196**), Andoar is a scapegoat whose death drives out Robinson's 'sin', that is, his colonising ethnocentrism, allowing him to begin a new life.

To the child who reads, the end of *Vendredi* may be no more, or no less, than a traditional fairytale ending: 'and they all lived happily ever after'. To the reader who is familiar with Tournier's other writings, a certain sexual ambiguity prevails. In other words, our reading of *Vendredi* is a function of the frameworks which we are able to bring to the text: able both in the sense of having certain information at our disposal, and equally in the sense that the text is open to these different readings. One striking feature of Tournier's text is that it makes us acutely aware of the reader's role, more specifically, of the constitutive nature of the reading act. As we saw, the protagonist Robinson comes to realise that there are different ways of seeing, that alternative perspectives exist, and this realisation prompts him to reflect upon his own point of view. We, as readers, come to see that *Vendredi* can be read, or interpreted, in several ways, that the text can be seen from different perspectives. Because the different interpretations which can be envisaged are not necessarily complementary, and cannot coexist simultaneously, we too are prompted to consider our own interpretive acts, aware of the fact that it is we ourselves, our knowledge, our point(s) of view which in a sense create the text.

*Vendredi* is not a text to which we can respond unequivocally, but rather, a ludic work which is shot through with ambiguity. The text holds up a mirror to our fluctuating responses: do we side with Robinson the twentieth-century Everyman, or take a stand against the loathsome coloniser? Faced with apparently contradictory structural models (linear or circular?), we question our own structuring activity. Furthermore, if we accept the open-ended nature of the text, we realise that it is we who are invited to write a conclusion, projecting forwards into a fictional future. The fantastic dimension of the text further highlights our role as readers, as we hesitate between interpretations of events. Are the mandrakes to be regarded as a sign that Robinson is undergoing a dehumanising process, entering a realm of mythical cooperation between animal and plant life, or is this supernatural interpretation untenable? Does Robinson truly stop ageing, or just feel that he does? Whenever we are faced with choice, or uncertainty, we are shaken out of our passive reading role and encouraged to reflect upon the reading process.

If the Robinson Crusoe story is a myth, and if readers recognise themselves in the mythical hero, where does this leave the reader of *Vendredi?* Defoe's readers could put down *Robinson Crusoe* and go out into the real world assured of the strength of the individual, the merits of hard work, the value of Christianity, and the supremacy of their culture. The novel had an exemplary function, and bore a didactic message which had a pragmatic outlet. Tournier's reader sees a man who has rejected the mainland values and turned his back on society. Is *Vendredi*, then, an escapist text promoting a Utopian vision which has no bearing on our lives? It might be seen as a product of the '60s, a text which won itself a cult, 'hippie' following. Robinson grows his hair long, advocates love, not war. The *extase solaire* bears all the hallmarks not only of the mystic's vision, but of the drug-induced hashish dream. And yet, the text still strikes a chord with today's reader. Sectors of society will always take a stand against the dominant ideology —today's New Age cult with its 'ecstasy' trips harks back to the hippie era of previous years. More than this, Robinson's rejection of society, his opting-out, perhaps appeals to a part of all of us. Although most of us choose to remain in society, and although *Vendredi* seems to advocate a way of life which is untenable in that society, the text touches that part of us which dreams of opting out, of 'getting away from it all', and in so doing, points to the deficiencies of a society which provokes such desires and dreams in its members, a hi-tech society of ambition and greed which has lost touch with the natural world, with spirituality, and with magic.

# References and Suggested Reading

Works in English and French are published in London and Paris, respectively, unless otherwise stated. The original year of publication, where relevant, is given between square brackets.

## References

Baudelaire, C.     'Le Peintre de la vie moderne', Gallimard, 'Bibliothèque de la Pléiade', vol. II, 1976.

Beauvoir, S. de     *Le Deuxième sexe,* vol. I. Gallimard, 'Folio', 1986 [1949].

Bouloumié, A.     'Deux thèmes chers au romantisme allemand: la mandragore et la harpe éolienne dans *Vendredi ou les limbes du Pacifique* de MichelTournier', *Recherches sur l'imaginaire,* XVII (1987), 163-78.

Defoe, D.     *The Life and Adventures of Robinson Crusoe.* Harmondsworth, Penguin Classics, 1985 [1719].

Eliade, M.     *Rites and Symbols of Initiation.* New York, Harper and Row, 1975.

————     *The Myth of the Eternal Return.* Arkana, 1989.

Freud, S.     *The Standard Edition of the Complete Works of Sigmund Freud* Hogarth Press, vol. XVI (Introductory Lectures on Psychoanalysis, Part III), 1963.

————     *On Metapsychology: The Theory of Psychoanalysis.* Pelican Freud Library, vol. 11, 1984.

Golding, W.     *Lord of the Flies.* Faber, 1973

Happold, F.C.     *Mysticism.* Penguin Books, 1988.

Hubbard, G.     *Quaker by Convincement.* Penguin Books, 1974.

MacLean, M.     'Michel Tournier as Misogynist (or not?): An Assessment of the Author's View of Femininity', *The Modern Language Review,* LXXXIII, 2 (1988), 322-31.

Petit, S.          'The Bible as Inspiration in Tournier's *Vendredi
                   ou les limbes du Pacifique*', *French Forum*, IX
                   (1984), 343-54.

Reeves, M.         *Joachim of Fiore and the Prophetic Future.*
                   S.P.C.K., 1986.

Sartre, J.-P.,     *La Nausée.* Gallimard, 'Folio', 1975 [1938].

Todorov, T.,       *The Fantastic: A Structural Approach to a
                   Literary Genre.* Ithaca, Cornell U.P., 1975
                   [*Introduction à la littérature fantastique*, 1970].

Tournier, M.       *Les Nouvelles littéraires*, 26 novembre 1970,
                   interview with Q. Ritzen.

_____         *Vendredi ou la vie sauvage.* Gallimard,'Folio
                   Junior', 1977 [1971].

_____         *Les Météores*, Gallimard, 'Folio', 1977 [1975].

_____         *Le Vent Paraclet*, Gallimard, 'Folio', 1981 [1977].

_____         'Qu'est-ce que la littérature?', interview with J.-J.
                   Brochier, *Le Magazine littéraire*, no. 79
                   (décembre 1981).

_____         *Le Médianoche amoureux.* Gallimard, 1989.

Wyss, J.D. / J.R.  *The Swiss Family Robinson* (Montolieu tr.).
                   Oxford, O.U.P. 'World's Classics', 1991 [1812].

## Suggested Reading

Bouloumié, A.      *Tournier: le roman mythologique, suivi de
                   questions à Tournier.* José Corti, 1988.

_____         *Michel Tournier: 'Vendredi ou les limbes du
                   Pacifique'.* Gallimard, 'Foliothèque', 1991.

Davis, C.          *Michel Tournier: Philosophy and Fiction,*
                   Oxford, Clarendon Press, 1988, pp. 9-33.

_____             'Michel Tournier's *Vendredi ou les limbes du
                   Pacifique:* a novel of beginnings', *Neophilologus*,
                   LXXIII (1989), 373-82.

Fergusson, K.      'Le Rire et l'absolu dans l'œuvre de Michel
                   Tournier', *Sud*, XVI, 61 (1986),. 76-89.

Genette, G.

*Palimpsestes: la littérature au second degré*, Seuil, 1982, ch. LXXV, pp. 418-25.

Hueston, P.

Interview with Tournier, *Meanjin*, 38 (1979), 400-405.

MacLean, M.

'Human Relations in the Novels of Tournier: Polarity and Transcendence', *Forum for Modern Language Studies*, XXIII, 3 (1987), 241-52.

Maulpoix, J.-M.

'Des limbes à la vie sauvage', *Sud*, XVI, 61 (1986), 33-42.

Merllié, F.

*Michel Tournier*. Belfond, 1988.

Petit, S.

*Michel Tournier's Metaphysical Fictions*, Amsterdam & Philadelphia, John Benjamins, 1991, pp. 1-23.

Purdy, A.

'From Defoe's *Crusoe* to Tournier's *Vendredi:* The Metamorphosis of a Myth', *Canadian Review of Contemporary Literature*, XI (1984), 216-35.

Roselo, M.

*L'In-difference chez Michel Tournier*. José Corti, 1990.

Sankey, M.

'Meaning through Intertextuality: Isomorphism of Defoe's *Robinson Crusoe* and Tournier's *Vendredi ou les limbes du Pacifique*', *Australian Journal of French Studies*, XVIII (1981), 77-88.

Sbiroli, L.S.

*Michel Tournier, la séduction du jeu*. Geneva, Slatkine, 1987.

Stirn, F.

*Tournier: 'Vendredi ou les limbes du Pacifique'*. Hatier, 'Profil d'une Œuvre', 1983.

Tournier, M.

*Le Coq de bruyère*, Gallimard, 'Folio', 1980 [1978].

Vierne, S.

*Rite, roman, initiation*. Grenoble, Presses Universitaires, 1987.

Worton, M.

'Écrire et ré-écrire: le projet de Tournier', *Sud*, XVI, 61 (1986), 52-69.